Books by Elizabeth-Ann Sachs

Just Like Always
Where Are You, Cow Patty?

Where Are You,
Cow Patty?

WHERE ARE YOU, COW PATTY?

Elizabeth-Ann Sachs

ATHENEUM　　1984　　NEW YORK

Many thanks to
my Schenectady Writers' Group
and the Breadloaf Family for all their help.
And a special thanks to Dr. Kathi Heiber
of the South Putnam Animal Hospital.

Library of Congress Cataloging in Publication Data

Sachs, Elizabeth-Ann.
Where are you, cow Patty?

SUMMARY: When her friends Courtney and Harold,
anxious about becoming teenagers, begin dating each
other, Janie feels left out, but then has a chance to
watch a calf being born, which helps her mature
in her own way.
[1. Friendship—Fiction. 2. Birth—Fiction]
I. Title.
PZ7.S1186Wh 1984   [Fic]   84-2950
ISBN 0-689-31057-9

Copyright © 1984 by Elizabeth-Ann Sachs
All rights reserved
Published simultaneously in Canada by
McClelland & Stewart, Ltd.
Composition by Maryland Line, Baltimore, Maryland
Printed and bound by Fairfield Graphics,
Fairfield, Pennsylvania
First Edition

To JAC III
who helped build
the second nest.

Where Are You,
Cow Patty?

1

Janie Tannenbaum decided to take the shortcut. She left the path and climbed over a wooden railed fence. Inching her way along the edge of the cliff, she refused to let herself look down the ravine. She knew there were trees at the bottom that had shattered from falling.

Janie grabbed for the slender tree that arched over the edge. "Are you coming, Harold?"

"You're nuts!" His voice came from somewhere up the trail. "Suppose that tree gives?"

"It never did before." Janie wrapped her arms around a limb, took a deep breath, then jumped into the air.

The tree sprang out and then down. Her

hands began to slip, and she felt herself fall. Janie's body dropped, and she barely touched down on the narrow ledge that jutted out below. It took her an instant to know she was safe.

"Janie?" Harold's round face peered over the cliff above.

"Yeah," was all she could say. The wind was out of her.

"Are you okay?"

"Of course," she snapped, but she leaned against the sun-warmed rock for assurance. Ten feet above her, the tree was still lurching up and down.

"I'll be right there."

Janie sat down slowly. "I'm okay, Harold." All about her, the mountains careened in a sickening green dance.

There was no response from above, and Janie lay back on the stone ledge. Her chest had stopped heaving, but her back ached. She rotated her shoulders and wiggled her behind. Even though she was still shaking, Janie knew she wasn't hurt. The only problem was, her old Indian leap wasn't the same any more.

"If you'd missed . . ." Harold panted. "You could have killed yourself." He had run down the trail along the shoulder of the cliff.

"Not a chance!" Janie got up. She wiped her hands on the back of her jeans.

"Well, you might have broken your back."

With the inside of his arm, he wiped sweat off his nose.

"Buzz off, Wazby!" Janie started on down the trail.

Harold shook his head but decided to say no more. Putting his green visor hat on backwards, he followed Janie around the first bend in the path.

When they reached the entrance to the town park, the bus was already there. "Window," Janie shouted before Harold could.

They paid their money and shoved past other picnickers toward the back of the bus. Janie took her favorite seat next to the window and right across from the rear door.

Harold slumped down beside her. "You know we only have twenty more days?"

"Don't remind me." Janie watched the blur of green trees as the bus rumbled down the mountain road.

Harold began playing with a hole in his black T-shirt. He was trying to make it bigger. "Janie, are you looking forward to being up at the junior high?"

She shook her head of dark red hair.

"Joel says it's pretty much the same old stuff."

"What's that mean?"

"Same subjects, same music director. He said the only real difference is you get to change classes and date girls."

"I'm not dating NO girls."

Harold made a face. "Sometimes you're weird, you know that!"

"You should talk, Wazby."

"Are you going out with boys is what I mean?"

Janie turned to look at him. "Are you kidding? Me?"

"Yeah." Harold rubbed his smooth chin. "You'd probably punch out the guy just for asking."

"Now you got it." Janie smiled. "You're not going to do junk like that, are you?"

"Yeah, I am."

"You are! But why?"

"Joel says you practically have to."

"Who cares what Joel says?"

"I do, sort of."

"Who are you going to ask?"

"I'm not sure yet."

"Why not?"

"It's not that easy, Janie. First, I have to figure out how you do it."

"Can't you just ask?"

"Suppose she says no, then what do I do?"

"Tell her she's dumb."

"That'll do me a lot of good. I just have to practice some more."

"What do you mean practice?"

"Not so loud, Janie."

"Well, what do you mean practice?"

"You know, so I can tell how it sounds."

"You do it out loud?"

"How else?"

"What do you say?"

"Just stuff."

"What kind of stuff? I want to hear."

"Not now, Janie." Harold peered at the people in the front seats.

"Why not? Pretend I'm the girl. Nobody will know the difference."

Harold glanced over his shoulder. There was no one behind them. "Okay." He lowered his voice. For a moment he was quiet. Then he put an arm around Janie.

"Hey, what's the big idea?"

"That's what you do. Sit still."

Janie scowled at him.

"Come on." Harold loosened his grip. "It won't kill you."

"Okay, then." Janie smiled. "My name's Marvella."

"What kind of dumb name is that? You think I'd ask out a girl with that name?"

"That's my name. You want to ask me out or not?"

"All right, all right." Harold took off his glasses. "Ahh . . . Marvella?"

"Yeah?" Janie pretended to be chewing gum.

"Listen, I was wondering if you'd like to go out with me to . . . to a movie?"

7

Janie batted her reddish eyelashes for a moment. "Which movie?"

"Ahh . . . well, I was thinking of the one in town."

"I already saw that." Janie patted her curly hair.

"How about the one at the mall?"

"My father said it was *too* dumb to be believed."

"Janie!" Harold's voice cracked.

"Well, I'm just trying to give you lots of practice."

"All right, all right! How about the movie near the library?"

"Yeah, sure, that sounds great."

"You mean you really will go out with me?"

"Harold, are you supposed to say that?"

"No, Janie will *you* go out on a date with me?"

"Huh?"

"You said you would."

"Are you crazy, Wazby?" Janie stood up and pulled the cord for the bus to stop. Harold stumbled out behind her.

As they crossed the street to their block, Harold kept saying, "Why not, Janie? Joel says we could practice."

Janie stopped in the middle of the road with her hands on her hips. "There is NO WAY I'm going out on a real date—or a practice either! See you later, Wazby!" She sprinted away toward home.

"Wait up," Harold yelled. "What's wrong with the idea?" He chased along the road calling after Janie.

"Hello?" Janie yanked open the screen door and let it slam behind her. Aiming her jacket at a doorknob, she headed through the empty kitchen. "Mom, I'm home."

"Up here, honey," Janie's mother called from the second floor.

Janie took the stairs two at a time. She stopped in the doorway to her mother's darkroom. "Can I come in?"

"Yup, door's open." Mrs. Tannenbaum turned off her desk lamp. She swung on the stool. "Did you have a good time?"

"Really great." Janie moved toward the old flowered couch.

"Guess who called?"

"I don't know." She plumped up the pillows. "Who?" she said, flopping into them.

"Take a wild guess."

"Frankenstein!"

Mrs. Tannenbaum scratched her dark red hair. "Okay, not so wild."

"I don't know." Janie put both hands behind her head and stretched her legs. "Tell me."

Janie's mother smiled. "Courtney Schaeffer called this afternoon."

"She did!" Janie sat upright. "What did she say? Is she home? Is she okay?"

"She sounded wonderful."

Janie hadn't heard from the girl she met in the hospital in over a year. She had started a letter to Courtney but never got around to finding the address. "Is her body cast off?"

"I forgot to ask, but she's home and wants you to go visit her."

"Wow! When?"

"Well, she mentioned this coming week. But that's no good, Janie."

"Why not?" Janie frowned.

Downstairs, the dog began to bark. Janie and her mother could hear the front door opening.

"Hello?" Mr. Tannenbaum called from the foot of the stairs. "Anybody home?"

"Hi, Daddy," Janie shouted.

"We're up here," Mrs. Tannenbaum yelled, then turned back to Janie. "I told Courtney to call tonight."

"Why can't I go?" Janie stood before her mother hands on hips.

"We have too much to do this week."

"What do you mean?"

"Hey"—Mr. Tannenbaum stuck his head in the door. "I'm starving; when's supper?"

"As soon as we cook it." Mrs. Tannenbaum stood up. "You can get the salad going while Janie and I make the hamburgers."

"I don't want to cook," Janie moaned.

"Here we go again." Mr. Tannenbaum rolled his dark brown eyes.

"What's that mean, dear?"

"Every meal around here has to be negotiated like a UN peace treaty. I work hard all day, you know."

"So do I, love!"

"Listen, I've been filming the garbage strike all day. I really need a shower. How about you two start and I do the clean-up detail afterwards?" He wiggled his dark eyebrows up and down.

Janie's mother said, "You're not trying to sneak out of helping, are you?"

"Me?" Mr. Tannenbaum slapped a hand over his heart. "Would I do a thing like that?" He disappeared quickly.

"Out you go, missy."

Janie puffed up her cheeks and blew out. "I hate cooking."

"Me too." Mrs. Tannenbaum steered Janie toward the door.

"But you're a mother. You're supposed to like it."

"Who told you that one?" Janie's mother flipped off the lights.

"What about Courtney?" Janie started down the stairs.

"Let's talk while we're cooking?"

"Grossness," Janie muttered.

2

———————◆———————

When dinner was finally over, Janie sat with her head between freckled hands. "Cow plops," she muttered.

"Janie, what's wrong?" Her father looked puzzled.

"I think it stinks."

"Let's talk about the problem." Helene Tannenbaum poured herself a second cup of coffee.

"The problem is"—Janie's tone was defiant—"you want me to be a slave." She glared at her mother.

"When you came home from the hospital,

you didn't want Daddy to pull out the wild blackberry patch."

"Well, the rabbits live there. I didn't want their home wrecked."

"Remember the deal we made?"

"Why can't we just let the birds have the berries this year?"

Mrs. Tannenbaum took a deep breath. "The berries are ripe. I need you to pick. You promised me you'd help."

"But you said yourself you hate canning."

"I do."

"So then, why?"

"Because I grew up on a farm, and food wasn't wasted. But that's not the point. We made a deal. I expect you to help."

Janie blew her frizzy bangs off her forehead. She could tell her mother wasn't going to give in.

"How come," her father said, putting down his cup, "no one has said anything about Courtney coming here?"

Even though Janie said, "Why would Courtney want to be on the chain gang?" she was pleased.

"That would certainly make life easier." Helene Tannenbaum glanced across the table at her husband. "Why didn't I think of that?"

"Brains!" He pointed to his head. "You have to have them."

Janie's smile suddenly faded. "But what if she can't?"

"Let's just wait and see." Andy Tannenbaum began picking up cups and plates. "And now since I came up with a solution, don't I deserve some help? Will all those in favor please say, 'Aye.' "

Opening a can of dog food later on, Janie heard Harold's wolf yowl. Fang made a dash for the front door. "It's open!" Janie yelled over the barking.

Fighting off the small brown poodle, Harold entered the kitchen. "Your dog is nuts. Why does he always go crazy when I come over? You'd think he'd know me by now!" Harold rested against the refrigerator.

"You're the only one he's not afraid of, Harold. He has to bark at you. It makes him feel like a real dog."

"Some honor!" Harold looked at the ceiling. "Hey, you want to go check out lovers' lane? We could spy on who's ever down there."

"You got lovers' lane on the brain." Janie perched on a countertop.

"Oh, very funny; since when are you a poet?"

"Well, what do you expect? All of a sudden that's all you talk about."

"How else am I supposed to find out? I can't ask my sister how she kisses Jimmy. She'd go nuts."

"Who cares, anyway?"

"Joel said we did it wrong that time. Now I got to find out what's right."

"Geeze, Harold, we were in third grade. We got sick from smoking cigars, too. Why can't we just go fishing now?"

"If I get my pole, will you walk the long way so we can see if there's anyone parking?"

Just then the phone rang. "That's for me. You check out the lovers, I'll meet you on the rocks." Janie jumped off the counter and yelled, "I'll get it, Mom!" She grabbed the yellow wall phone. "City Morgue! You stab'um, we slab'um."

"Is this 783-2 . . . ?"

"Courtney!"

"Janie?"

"Yeah, hi!" Sprawling on the kitchen floor, Janie heard the door slam.

"I wasn't sure I had the right number."

"I always do that. How *are* you?"

"I'm fine, Janie. How are you?"

"I'm great! Terrific! Wow, is this neat. My mother said you're home."

"I've been home awhile."

"Hey, Courtney, I'm sorry I didn't write back the last time. I got sort of busy and . . ."

"That's okay."

"You're not mad?"

"Of course not."

Hearing Courtney's voice brought back all

kinds of memories for Janie. The hospital room they had shared, those first scary nights when they whispered back and forth in the dark.

"Janie, are you there?"

"Yeah. Are you still in the cast?"

"No. It's off finally."

"Super, no more cement clothing."

"Janie, is your back okay?"

"Yeah, I do whatever I want. Even the stuff the doctors said not to. Goodbye scoliosis!"

"You sound exactly the same; I was afraid you'd changed."

"Nope. Did you sneak out of the hospital for ice cream again?"

"Oh, Janie, I could only do that with you around. I missed you so much after you left."

"I bet no one else did." Janie remembered the blind date they had schemed between the doctor and the nurse, and the pigeons who had almost died from hospital food they had thrown out their windows.

"That's not true, at all. They were still talking about our love questionnaire when I went back for x-rays in June."

"No kidding." Janie also remembered how they had bribed the nurse into eating the gross hospital food while they lived on goodies from her grandmother. It seemed like a very long time ago. "How long were you there after I left?"

"A couple of months. I had to have another

operation and I was real slow in physical therapy."

"Yeah, that was the pits." Talking to Courtney brought back the bad times, also. "Listen," Janie said, pushing the past aside, "do you think you could come here?"

"I was going to ask you, Janie."

"I know, but I got to do some junk around here."

"I'll have to ask my mother."

"I'll hang on."

"She's not home now."

"Why don't you just leave her a note and take a bus or something."

Courtney laughed. "I can't do that. I'll have to call you tomorrow."

"Just make sure you get here. You can stay forever."

"I can't wait to see you again, Janie."

"Yeah, it'll be so neat."

"Just like old times."

"Right."

"I better go; this is long distance."

"Okay."

"Oh, Janie, I don't want to say goodbye."

"Me, either."

"I better I guess."

"Okay, count to three. Then, we'll both hang up together."

"Bye, see ya' soon." Janie yelled, then slammed down the phone.

"Wow! Terrific," she whooped moments later going out the garage door.

"What is?" Harold eased himself off the stone wall.

With fishing pole in hand Janie started down the driveway. "I thought you were spying on lovers' lane?"

"It's no fun alone." He hurried to keep up with Janie. "So what's so terrific?"

"That was Courtney on the phone."

"Who's she?"

"You know, I told you. The girl I shared a room with in the hospital. The one who did the magical stuff." Janie crossed the dirt road.

"Magical stuff! In a hospital?"

"Yeah, remember those fantasy books about Greno she gave me?"

"No."

Janie and Harold made their way into the narrow strip of woods that ran along the lake, across from her house. As they reached the mossy bank, Janie said, "Well, she's coming here for a visit."

Harold put his tackle box down on the rocks. "Is this that girl who thinks she can talk in your head?"

"Right. And not only that, Harold . . ." Janie baited her hook. ". . . she can see things that aren't even there. We did it all the time."

"What good is that?"

"That's what I said when I heard about her Greno club, but it was great."

"I don't believe any of it."

Janie threw out her line. "I could show you; I even remember."

Harold shook his head. "What I want to know is, are you and her going to spend the week looking at stuff that's not there?"

"No, we'll all hang around together."

"Bet you she can't even walk through the woods without making noise."

"Hey, Harold, quit worrying." Janie pounded his shoulder. "You'll love her."

"Yeah, sure. My last week," Harold muttered.

"You really have to go to that camp?"

"Yeah, my parents are making me."

"Why don't you throw that violin out a window?"

"My mother'd kill me. It was her father's."

"I never even heard of a music camp. What do you do there?"

"Play the violin all day, I guess."

"Don't you get to swim?"

"I don't know."

"But what about your harmonica?"

"This camp's only for serious violinists."

"I think harmonica music is serious."

"Well, they don't."

"You could play all crazy when you get there."

"Why would I do that?"

"Maybe they'd kick you out then."

"And then what would I do? My parents would disown me."

"No, they wouldn't."

"You don't have Jeanette and George for parents."

Janie thought for a moment. "You could hide out in the woods, and I'd bring you food every day."

Janie couldn't hear what Harold mumbled to himself. Watching the last of the light disappear from the sky, she thought about how super it would be seeing Courtney again. There was so much she wanted to show her.

"Want to go?" Harold reeled in his line. "We're not catching anything."

"Yeah." Janie slammed the lid on her box of tackle and lures.

When they were both ready, Harold started down the path. He stopped suddenly and faced Janie. "Want to hold hands going back?"

"WAZBY!" Janie bellowed. "What *is* your problem?"

3

"Get away from me!" Janie shouted at the red glass bird. She threw a rock, but it kept coming. "Get away!" she roared. Janie turned and fled down the long dark tunnel. She could feel the bird's breath on her back. The hall went on and on with no light at the end.

"Janie," a voice called. "Oh, Janie, wake up!" It was a nice voice, a friendly voice.

Janie opened her eyes. The frog lamp glowed softly over her head.

"Hey, honey." Mrs. Tannenbaum's hand rested on Janie's shoulder. "You okay?"

Janie rolled over and rubbed her eyes. "I was having a nightmare."

"You were shouting at someone, giving them a terrible time."

"Was I yelling?" Janie pushed the covers back and sat up.

"At first we thought someone was really in here. Mrs. Tannenbaum sat on the edge of Janie's bed.

"Oh, Mom." Janie leaned against her pillows. "I remember now. A big bird with army boots and a yellow hat was after me. He wanted a kiss."

"Good thing I woke you." She brushed the hair off Janie's damp forehead.

Janie looked out the window. "Think Harold heard me?"

"He could have. Want to read for a while, before you go back to sleep?"

"I'm not sleepy anymore."

"You know, I'm not either, now." Mrs. Tannenbaum looked at the clock. "And it's the middle of the night."

"I feel like playing. Want to go have a quick game of catch?"

"I don't think so, Janie. I'm not in the mood for baseball. Besides," she said, laughing, "the Wazbies think we're crazy as it is. Harold's father would probably call the police."

Janie giggled. "We could do something quiet, like fishing."

"How about reading?"

"Nah, I wanna DO something!"

Just then Janie's poodle jumped onto the bed. Mr. Tannenbaum followed him into the room. "I want you to know this is some kind of watchdog. He was barking from under the couch."

"Oh, brave Fang!" Janie scratched the dog's head. He thumped his stumpy tail on the quilt.

"Well . . ." Mr. Tannebaum yawned. ". . . I'm going back to bed. Some of us have to work for a living." He kissed Janie. "If you ladies will excuse me." The dog followed him down the hall.

Janie waited till they were gone. "Is Daddy mad cause I woke him?"

"No, just grumpy about work. His other cameraman quit. Janie, my feet are cold. Can I crawl in with you?"

"Sure." Janie scooted over, making room under the covers.

"Oh, Janie! I forgot! Mrs. Schaeffer phoned after you went to bed. Courtney refused to go to sleep until her mother called back."

"What did she say? Can Courtney come?"

"Yes; Sunday afternoon."

"For how long?"

"Till Friday."

"I wish it could be longer."

"We can always invite her again if you both have a good time?"

"What do you mean *if*?"

"Sometimes it's hard to meet a friend in one place and then get together in another."

"Not with Courtney."

"It's been a year and a half since you've seen her, Janie. You've changed; she probably has too."

"No way; it'll be fantastic!"

"I hope so." They both sat thinking separate thoughts about Courtney, until Janie's mother said, "You know, this is some room! I never sat in your bed before and looked at it. Usually, I just close the door on my way to the studio."

Janie leaned against her mother. "Yeah, I did it all myself. Look how much stuff I have in here."

"What's that heap on the desk?"

"Sachet guts. We learned how to make them in school. I was going to do a million and sell them for a new bike. But I got bored sewing."

"And that pile?"

Janie looked at her other twin bed. "Oh, that's how I figure out what to wear. With all my clothes mixed-up, I can see what colors look good together."

Janie's mother nodded. "You probably should make some space in here for Courtney."

Janie studied her room. "Looks okay to me. I'll just clear a path to the other bed."

Mrs. Tannenbaum put her feet on the floor. "Come on, Janie. You said you wanted to *do* something."

Janie wrinkled her face. "You look like you're planning something I'm sure to hate."

24

"Let's just clear off the bed so Courtney doesn't have to sleep out in the hall. Besides, I want to see what you have in that closet."

Janie fell back on her pillows. She pulled the covers up over her head. "Now I really am having a nightmare."

On Saturday afternoon Janie shoved the heap of books, old shoes, and hangers under the bed where they had always been. With her snake skins back in the corner, the room felt almost like hers again. With any luck, Janie figured, her mother wouldn't notice she'd put her stuff back where it belonged. Shoving the two birds' nests in the closet, she heard Harold's bike bell jangle outside.

"Janie?"

She moved to the window. "Yeah?"

In the front yard Harold straddled his bicycle with both legs stretched out. "Can you come out?"

"Not right now."

"What are you doing?"

"Fixing up my room."

Harold squinted up at Janie. "When will you be done?"

"Later, why?"

"Want to bike into town for an ice cream?"

"Sure."

"I'll pay."

"How come, Harold?"

"Just like that."

"Since when? Hey, you're not trying to get me out on a date, are you?" Janie watched the sun glinting on Harold's glasses. She couldn't see his eyes.

"Joel says I did it all wrong yesterday. He said you're supposed to ask the girl what she wants to do."

"Harold!" Janie pounded on the wooden sill. "It's got nothing to do with what Joel says. Besides, you'd hate it if we went out on a date."

Harold shaded his eyes with one hand and frowned up at Janie. "How do you know?"

"You just would, Harold."

"You're crazy. What's there to hate?"

Janie pressed her forehead against the screen. "How much you want to bet you wouldn't hate dating?"

"You want to bet on something like that?"

"Yeah, why not?"

Harold crossed his arms over his narrow chest. "Okay, if you're right, you can buy anything on the menu."

"Even a Sweet Sixteen?"

"Two of them, if I *really* hate it."

Thirty-two scoops of ice cream sounded like a pretty good gamble to Janie. "You're on, Harold. Go break your piggy bank."

"Hey, what do I get if you're wrong?"

"I don't know. What do you want?"

"How about another date?"

"No way!" Janie straightened up.

"Then NO deal, Janie."

In her mind, Janie could see all that ice cream with hot fudge and nuts. "Okay," she moaned. "Two dates, if I lose."

"When do you want to go?" Harold put one foot on the bike pedal.

"Tonight, if it's a real date."

"Janie, you know I'm not allowed to bike into town after dark. It has to be before supper."

"How about five minutes?"

"Great, I'll just wait." Harold began making great sweeping circles in the front yard.

As he moved away from the house, Janie thought of something. "Hey, Harold! Come back a sec."

Harold skidded to a stop in the grass. "Now what?" He pushed the bicycle backwards up the lawn.

"I need more time than that."

"What for?"

Janie thought for a moment. "I have to do my hair."

"What are you talking about?" Squinting up at her, Harold said, "We're just going for ice cream."

"Yeah, I know. Let's make it three o'clock."

"But it's only one o'clock! Since when do you DO your hair?"

Janie moved away from the window. Harold yelled her name a couple more times, but she didn't answer. With hands on hips, Janie stood thinking. She wandered down the hall toward the bathroom, knowing it was not going to be easy to change Harold's mind.

On the sink were her mother's perfumes. She sniffed one and gagged. Holding her nose, Janie gave herself a heavy squirt.

Next she yanked open the middle drawer of the vanity. Different colored bottles and pencils rolled forward. "I dare you," Janie said, looking up at the mirror. Her reflection shook its head.

Janie smiled. "Okay, then, I double dare you." This time the answer wasn't no.

Janie pulled open all the drawers. "Eenie, meenie, minie, mo." With her eyes closed she pulled out a handful of different kinds of makeup. First, she put on a layer of what she thought was rouge. It was almost brown against her freckles. She also used a thick coating of lavender on her eyelids. Some became crusted in her eyelashes, so she rummaged around till she found the black mascara to cover it.

Janie had a hard time figuring which way the false eyelashes went on. But she finished off her face with a big black heart painted beside her lower lip.

Janie stood back with one hand on her hip

and surveyed her work. With her head thrown back and her flat chest sticking out, she said, "Kiss me, you fool." But she sneezed; her eyes were beginning to water.

"Don't chicken out now, kid." She pointed a finger at the stranger in the mirror. "We can each get an ice cream."

Back in her room, Janie could not find much that looked like what she thought a girl was supposed to wear on a date. What she needed was that dress Grandma Tannenbaum had sent from Florida, the one with the green palm trees and pink flamingos. That gross thing would be perfect.

Janie climbed into the hot, stuffy attic where her mother stored old clothes. She found the hand-painted dress, but it was too small. The waist, when she struggled into it, was almost up to her armpits.

"I need something really putrid." Janie sneezed as she opened the wooden trunk. "Oh, wow! This'll be beautiful with my purple sweat shirt." Janie pulled on a black and red polka-dot mini-skirt.

She opened the door to a metal storage closet and flipped through layers of suits and coats. There was nothing interesting to wear and it was too hot for the bunny cape. "You poor thing." She petted the fur.

Down on the floor of the closet, among the

old shoes, Janie found exactly what she was looking for. With her orange and green socks on, Janie stepped into a pair of gold lamé spiked heels.

Outside, the doorbell rang faintly. Fang was barking. Janie clomped down the attic stairs trying not to fall out of the shoes. The bell chimed again.

"Hold your horses," she yelled. "I'm coming, already!"

The bell rang a third time. Janie flung the front door open. She threw her arms around Harold's neck.

"Are you crazy?" Harold struggled to break free.

Janie steadied herself in the golden shoes and looked Harold in the eyes. "You said you wanted to go out on a real date, didn't you?"

"Yeah, but . . ."

"Deal's a deal, Harold."

"Listen, here's the money." Harold shoved a hand in his back pocket. "I think you'll have to go it alone."

"Boy, and I was looking forward to my first date."

"You wouldn't really go into town looking like that, would you?"

"Want to make a little bet?"

"Forget it." Harold started to leave.

"Hey, wait, I'll go change."

"Now, how long is it going to take?"

"Two seconds." Janie stumbled back in the house. Her skin was really beginning to itch.

"Hey, look!" Harold pointed to the wooden bridge as they came up the road. He and Janie were pushing their bicycles back from the ice cream shop.

As they came closer, Janie read the purple letters sprayed on the white rails. " 'Where are you, cow patty?' That's weird."

"Wow, they covered the whole railing." Harold left his bike by the side of the road with Janie's.

She touched the paint. "Look at this stupid cow face." Some of the paint came away on her finger.

"They must have just done it." Harold watched Janie rubbing paint off on her shorts. "Wonder what it means?"

"Who knows? It's dumb, though. Hey, you want to climb down under the bridge?"

"The water's still too high, Janie." Harold went back for his bike.

"Aww, come on, Harold. How come you never want to do fun stuff anymore?"

"I don't know . . . it's babyish."

Suddenly there was the sound of brakes squealing and a great squawking noise. Then Janie and Harold saw an old maroon car speeding around the other side of the lake.

"Come on!" Janie shouted as she dropped her

bike in the dirt again. When she reached the narrow bend in the road, the air was filled with white feathers.

Catching up to Janie, Harold gasped, "Pillow fight!"

"Harold, look! Mr. Ransom's goose!" There on the side of the road was a bloody heap.

"Oh, disgust!" Harold stopped in the middle of the road.

Janie knelt beside the bird. "Poor Roger."

"Geez, his guts are coming out."

"Harold"—Janie looked up at his pale face—"go tell my father to call Ransoms'."

"It's too late, Janie. Look how much blood he's lost."

"No!"

"Janie. . . ."

"He's still alive, Harold. Maybe we can save him."

Harold got his bike and headed up the road toward Janie's house. After he was gone, Janie moved closer to the blood-spattered bird.

"Hang in there, Roger. You'll be okay." Cautiously, she stroked the white head with one finger.

It seemed like a very long time before Janie heard footsteps running down the road again. "Janie, are you all right?" It was her father's voice.

"It's Ransoms' pet goose. Someone hit him."

Farther up the road Janie could see white-haired Mr. Ransom hurrying toward them. He was carrying a blue blanket.

Janie stepped aside when the plump man bent down to wrap the bird up. "Oh Roger," he crooned, holding the bird like a baby, "I keep telling you those cars are bigger than you."

"Want us to call the vet?" Janie looked at the ground rather than Mr. Ransom's blue eyes.

"Mrs. R. did already." The old man started up the hill, then turned around. "Thanks," he said looking straight at Janie. He didn't wait for an answer.

Janie moved closer to her father. "You think Roger will die, Dad?"

"I don't know. He looked pretty badly messed up."

She moved her hands deep into her pockets. "I didn't even know what to do to stop the bleeding.

Mr. Tannenbaum put his arm around Janie's shoulder. "You did the right thing—getting help."

"Was Mr. Ransom mad when you called?"

"He was upset. Why would he be mad?"

"From that day Harold and I tried to horse-back ride his cows around the pasture."

"That was years ago, Janie."

"Yeah, even before the hospital. You think he's forgotten?"

"I'm sure he has."

Janie nodded. What her father said made

sense. She hoped Mr. Ransom didn't still think she was as mean as he'd said. "Hey, what happened to Harold?"

"He said he had to go practice for a music lesson. But he looked a little green to me."

"Yeah, for a second I thought he was going to throw up." Janie looped her arm around her father's waist.

When they reached her bicycle by the side of the road, Janie bent to pick it up. "Dad, when did you start asking girls out?"

"What?" Her father laughed.

"How old were you?"

"About forty, I'd say."

"Daddy!" Janie elbowed his ribs. "Come on!"

"Let me think a minute." They headed for the graveled driveway that led up to the house. Off in the distance was the sound of violin music.

4

"Where is she?" Janie paced back and forth in the parking lot. "I can't stand waiting another minute."

Mr. Tannenbaum sat on the hood of the old red Jeepster. "Want me to film her arrival for the six o'clock news?"

"Could you really? Have you got a camera here?"

"I was only teasing, Janie."

"Boy, I thought you meant it."

Janie was interrupted by a voice on the loud-speaker. "Attention, the Mill Cross Express bound for points north is now arriving on track one. Attention, the Mill . . ."

"Come on!" Janie rushed for the main gate. "She's here!"

Janie took the stairs two at a time. She reached the platform as the train slowed to a complete stop. Frantically, she looked around. Passengers were getting on and off; luggage was handed down.

Only when Mr. Tannenbaum waved both arms did Janie see a blonde girl in a flowing pink dress step down. Janie watched as her father hugged her. Even at a distance Janie could see that Courtney was prettier than she remembered. "Courtney!" Janie raced along the station platform, dodging passengers, jumping suitcases. "You made it!"

"Bear hugs! Bear hugs!" Courtney opened her arms.

"Greno!" Janie hollered as she crashed into her friend.

"Baseball." Courtney squeezed Janie hard.

Janie stood back. "You hair, it's all grown out."

"I had it styled." Courtney turned her head sideways. "Do you like it?"

"Yeah, but you sure look different. Fancier or something."

"You're taller, I think, Janie."

"Hey." Janie laughed. "We've never seen one another in regular clothes, just pajamas. No wonder we look different."

"Come on, girls." Mr. Tannenbaum picked

up three pieces of designer luggage. "Let's get going."

Janie grabbed the shopping bag and the cardboard box. "What's all of this stuff?" She shifted the box around in her arms and started up the stairs.

"I didn't know what we would do."

"Did you bring a bathing suit?"

"No, I never thought of that."

"Well, you can borrow one of mine."

Courtney hesitated halfway up the stairs. "I'm not a swimmer, Janie."

Over her shoulder, Janie said, "Swimming's a snap. I can teach you."

"Look how I put the furniture. Janie dropped the lavender suitcase in the middle of the room.

Courtney stopped in the doorway. "It's even better than you described it in the hospital."

Janie jumped on her bed. "You should have seen it yesterday. In honor of your visit, I moved the caterpillar cemetery out from under your bed."

"What's that?" Courtney pointed to a dead tree branch nailed to an orange wall.

"A wasp's nest. But it's empty, so you don't have to worry."

"Good thing." Courtney opened her luggage. "Bugs give me the creeps. Can I hang my skirts in your closet?"

"Yup. See, we each have a night stand next

to our bed, like in the hospital. I wanted to get bedpans, but my mother wouldn't let me."

"That's okay with me." Courtney handed Janie a small package. "That's for you."

"Hey, thanks. But I don't have anything for you."

"That's okay. I thought of this as I was going out the door."

Janie unwrapped the pale green tissue paper. "It's pretty." She held up a black snail shell on a golden chain.

"Everyone on Greno carried them."

"Do I wear it?"

"Yes. See, I have one, too." Courtney pulled aside the collar of her dress.

"Does everyone in your Greno club wear them?" Janie fastened the clasp.

"There is no more club. When I came home from the hospital, no one cared about it anymore."

"Why? What happened?"

Courtney sat down on the other twin bed. For a moment she played with her antique ring. "While we were in the hospital, my friend Marguerite and a girl named Shelly got to be best friends."

"Did they leave you out?"

"Not exactly, but my mother says that three's a crowd."

"But that's not fair."

"Then they started meeting boys in the playground after school."

"So . . . ?"

"Well . . . they just wanted to be with them. I felt strange being there."

Janie sat quietly. "Something like that happened to me. Harold and I used to be best friends. . . ." She looked up at Courtney. "Before I met you. He's been different ever since I got home. He hangs around with this older kid, Joel."

"Is Harold your boyfriend?"

"No WAY!"

"Well, if you don't have a boyfriend yet, I won't feel so bad!"

"Not you too." Janie let out a groan.

A puzzled look crossed Courtney's face.

"Harold's been bugging me lately about going out."

"Really?"

"Yeah, I had my first date, yesterday." Janie laughed remembering it.

"But I thought you said he wasn't your boyfriend."

"It was only a goof. Not for real. Hey, let's go swimming. You can finish unpacking later."

"Janie, I don't really like the water."

"Why not? It's about the only exercise the doctors said we should do."

"I know, but I'm always afraid I'll drown."

"Listen, why don't you let me show you."

"Not today. I'm really tired from the trip."

"Okay, I know a place we can go."

"Is it far?"

"Just up the road."

"Will your mother mind if I leave things hanging around your room?"

"We'll just close the door." Janie waved Courtney out of her room.

"Come on," said Janie. "We're almost there." She led the way up an overgrown path that went through the abandoned apple orchard.

"Where are you taking me?" Courtney's face was flushed from trying to keep up.

"You'll see." Janie climbed over the stone wall and waited.

Courtney paused to catch her breath. "Janie, I don't know if I can make it."

"Sure you can." Janie started back to help. "Put one foot in that hole right there." She pointed to a place where a large rock had fallen out of the wall. "Now, take my hand."

Awkwardly, Courtney lifted herself over the wall and back down the other side. "Thanks. Could we rest a minute?"

"Not here." Janie turned around.

Courtney wiped the dampness off her upper lip. "How much further?"

"Not much." Janie continued down the path till she came to a hedge of green. There she broke through and held the branches back for Courtney.

Before them was a wooden bridge that led over a shallow, muddy pond. Beyond the water was an old red barn with one wall missing. Wild ducks played in the water and nestled in the exposed loft.

"It's magical." Courtney stopped on the slatted bridge.

"Wait till you see the loft."

"Let's stay here. This is wonderful." Courtney gazed up at the huge willows.

"It's really neat inside. There's still a pig sty and horse stalls."

Courtney wrinkled up her nose. "It looks dangerous in there. I'd rather just sit by the water."

"Okay." Janie flopped down near a tree. She watched as Courtney picked a spot on the grass.

"Is there any poison ivy around?"

"Not here." Janie leaned back on the warm earth. With her eyes closed to the sun, Janie laughed at herself. How could she have forgotten? This was Courtney-Ann. Of course she wouldn't want to go into a smelly old barn.

"This is gorgeous, Janie. Do you come here much?"

Janie opened her eyes. "Not anymore."

"But it's so beautiful. Why not?"

Janie sat up. She wrapped her arms around her bare legs. "When I first got home from the hospital I used to."

"After your cast came off?"

"Yeah." Janie ran the tips of her fingers over the soft grass.

"I couldn't even stand up when they took mine off."

Watching the water, Janie ripped a clump of grass out of the ground. "All the time I was in bed, I used to dream of running. It would be almost like flying. When the cast came off, I couldn't even walk." A breeze whispered in the willows. Janie shivered.

"Then no one told you either—I mean about not being able to walk right away?"

Janie nodded without looking at Courtney. "So this was my big exercise. At first I could just about make it here." She flung the handful of sod away.

"You know what, Janie? All that time I was learning to walk and you weren't there, I imagined you running up and down the halls."

"Nope." Janie looked out at the still pond.

Courtney moved closer to Janie. "I never thought you would have had a hard time."

Janie shrugged her shoulders. More than anything, she wished she could forget about those first few days after the cast had come off. Her legs had been so wobbly and weak.

"In physical therapy"—Courtney looked at Janie—"I kept telling myself I had to be strong enough to play baseball with you when I came here."

42

Janie smiled. "We talked about that right before my operation, didn't we? I forgot about
that."

"I couldn't, Janie." The breeze wiffled through
Courtney's hair. "That was the last time I saw
you."

"I remember."

"Janie, what did you do after the doctors said
you didn't have to go back to the hospital
again?"

Janie laughed to herself remembering. "You
really want to know?"

Courtney nodded.

"I went over to Harold's house and rang the
bell. When he came out, I beat him up."

Courtney blinked. "Why?" she said.

"He and I always did stuff like that. I just
wanted to make sure everything was back to
normal. Abruptly, Janie stood up. "Come on,
let's go. I want to show you the cows."

Janie started down the road before Courtney
could ask more questions. She didn't want to
hang around talking anymore.

"Can we come back again, Janie? I want to
pick some of these flowers." Courtney trailed
behind.

"Maybe," Janie shouted back as she climbed
through the wooden fence.

5

"Who's for another piece of pie?" Mr. Tannenbaum looked around the dining room.

"Well, I wouldn't want it to go to waste." Janie slid her dish across the table.

"How about you, Courtney?"

"No, thank you."

"Me either," Mrs. Tannenbaum said.

Just then the bell rang. Fang started barking.

"You know who that is, Fang. Get him!" Janie and the dog raced through the kitchen. She shoved open the front door. "Hey, Harold! Come on in."

"Want to go fishing?"

"We're finishing dessert. And it's my night to clean up. We could meet you after."

"What do you mean *we*?"

"Courtney's here."

"Already!"

"Yeah, come on in. I want you to meet her."

"Maybe tomorrow, Janie." Harold ran his fingers through his hair.

"Come on, come on." She grabbed his arm. "Besides, my father made the greatest blackberry pie."

"Oh, all right." Harold tucked the front of his shirt in. He followed Janie through the kitchen and into the next room.

"Courtney." Janie leaned on the dining room chair. "This is Harold, my pal since kindergarten."

"Hello." Courtney smiled up at him. "It's nice to meet you." She blushed.

"And this"—Janie made a sweeping gesture —"is Courtney-Ann Schaeffer. High Queen of the Fantasy Club!"

Harold blushed up to his sandy hairline. "Lo, there." His chin jerked up slightly.

Courtney looked down at her hands. Neither one knew what else to say.

Mr. Tannenbaum cleared his throat. "So, Harold, how's the fishing been?"

"Lousy." Harold avoided looking at Courtney as he helped himself to a huge piece of pie and ice cream. He concentrated on his plate.

"Janie," her mother said, "since it's Courtney's first night, you can skip helping. Why don't the three of you find something to do?"

"We'll probably go out."

"I want you back in the house by dark, Janie."

"We will be, don't worry."

The sun was dropping behind the lake when Courtney, Janie, and Harold went out the front door.

"It's so beautiful out." Courtney took a deep breath. "And it smells wonderful."

Janie stuck a blade of grass in her mouth.

"Hey," Harold said, "want to go check out the wall?"

Janie looked at Courtney. "Want to?"

"What's the wall?"

"It's this place Harold and I hang out. You go through the woods, down to the lake."

Courtney studied the sky. "It's getting dark, I don't think so, Janie."

"Geeze," Harold grumbled. "There's a trail."

"Why don't you two go, Janie. I'd rather sit here and watch the stars come out."

"Nah, that's okay. Let's stick together." Janie sat cross-legged in the grass. "Harold, we could go tomorrow. Do you have your harmonica?"

Harold put his hands in his pockets. "I'd rather go down to the lake."

"But we need flashlights now."

"So, I'll get one."

"It's better during the day."

Harold dropped down on the grass. He lay back, arms behind his head.

"What kind of wall is it, Janie?" Courtney sat on the stoop.

"All the land around here used to be called Blackberry Farms. Supposedly, the lake is where the pasture was, and the stone walls go right into the water. You know that barn we saw?"

"Yes."

"That was part of it, too. There's a pasture out there under water."

"You mean that lake covers an entire pasture?"

"Yup!"

"That sounds like something from Greno."

"Hey, I never thought of that. Would you tell Harold—?"

"HAR-old." A voice cut across the twilight. "Mom says you have to come in now."

Harold grumbled under his breath.

"Let's go to the wall tomorrow. Okay?" Janie said.

"Sure, sure."

"Bye, Harold." Janie called after him.

Courtney was quiet. She seemed to be looking at the stars.

* * *

"Good night," Janie yelled to her parents. She shut the door to her room and kicked her sneakers toward the closet. "Boy, was Harold ever weird tonight!"

Courtney sat on the edge of her bed. "I feel bad that you didn't go with him."

"We can always do that." Janie dropped her jeans in a heap.

"Harold really wanted to, Janie." Courtney unlaced her green cloth sandals.

"Well, I wanted to stay with you. And besides we always sit on the stoop like that. I don't know what his problem was tonight."

"I know." Courtney pulled her pajamas out of the suitcase.

"You do?"

"He doesn't like me, Janie."

"How could he not like you? He doesn't even know you."

"I think it's because . . ." Courtney struggled with her words. "Because of my back."

Janie sat beside Courtney. "What do you mean? I have the same back as you, and he's my friend."

"He knows I have something wrong with me."

"That's crazy! There is nothing wrong with you."

"But, you said yourself, he's not your boyfriend."

"But *I* don't want a boyfriend!"

Courtney went to the closet and hung up her skirt. She said in a very quiet voice, "I do, Janie."

"Why?" Janie grimaced. "What for?"

Courtney unbuttoned her blouse, slowly. "Marguerite makes it sound so nice."

"Sounds yucky to me." Janie shook her head. She looked at Courtney standing in her pajama bottoms, with her blouse opened. "When did you start wearing a bra?"

"I just got it."

Janie looked down at her orange T-shirt. "Well, I'm planning on being flat-chested forever. Did you get your period yet?"

"No, did you?"

"No, but I'm in no rush."

"Really? I'm afraid I'll be sixteen before mine starts. Some girls—"

"What's your scar from the operation like?"

"Disgusting."

"Is it all red, still?"

"It's really ugly."

"If I showed you mine, could I see yours?"

"Oh Janie . . . I don't like anyone to see my back."

"Not even me? The kid with the same scoliosis, same operation, same cast?"

"Janie . . . ?"

"Besides," Janie persisted, "it's so hard to tell what it all looks like in a mirror."

"But, I don't want to see."

"Well, I do."

Courtney nodded. "Only because it's you, Janie. Slowly, she turned around and pulled the back of her blouse up.

Janie stood behind Courtney. "It's redder than mine, but that's 'cause it's newer. But you know what? It's a wonderful scar."

"How can you say that?" Courtney looked straight ahead. "It's awful."

"No way." Janie put her hand on Courtney's back. "Can you feel my fingers?"

"Yes."

"It runs between your shoulder blades like a river between two mountains and then down." Janie traced the scar.

Tears welled up in Courtney's eyes. "Only you, Janie . . ." She turned to hug her friend. "Could I see yours?"

"Yup." Janie faced the window. She felt Courtney's cool fingers on her spine. "Tell me about mine."

"Yours has almost an 'S' shape to it."

"Does it flow like a river too?"

"One that bends on its way through the mountains. Janie?" Courtney moved along side of her friend. "Does it bother you that they put a metal rod inside your back?"

"Yeah."

"I get scared whenever I think what they did to straighten me out."

"Especially that they wired my spine to . . ." Janie touched her hips.

"Can you ever feel it, Janie? I know what the doctors said, but sometimes I'm sure I do."

Janie bit her lip. "I think so, but the worst part is I don't feel like I used to."

Courtney wrapped an arm around Janie's waist. "I try to tell myself it's like when you straighten a bent tree with a stake."

Janie sighed. "I don't know what you mean."

"Well, you put a stake next to a tree and pull them together with a rope."

"My mother has a tree like that in her studio."

"I pretend the wires are beautiful ribbons, pulling me straight."

"I hate thinking about it."

"But you know what Janie, no matter where we go for our entire lives, even if we hate one another when we grow up, we'll always have something that's the same."

Quietly, Janie returned Courtney's hug. Then, without a word, she flipped off the lights. The two stood looking out at darkness as they once had from a hospital window. Finally Janie whispered, "Greno may be gone, but you and I have our own special club now."

6

Not long after daybreak, Janie opened her eyes, thinking about Harold. In the other bed, Courtney was curled up fast asleep. Janie grabbed her clothes and crept downstairs.

Dressed, she took worms and cheese out of the refrigerator. Super breakfast, Janie thought, heading out to the road. Early mornings were her favorite time. She and Harold and the ducks in the marsh always began the day together. Janie cut through the woods and walked along the uncleared shore.

"Hi-ya, Harold." She sat on the rocks. "Catch anything yet?"

"Nope."

"Want any worm bait?"

"Didn't expect to see you."

"Courtney's sleeping. I thought I'd fish with you."

"Swell."

"What's bugging you?"

Harold finally turned around and looked over at Janie. "Your girl friend, that's what. How come she doesn't want me around?"

"What?" Janie said, startled.

"She just wanted to get rid of me last night. I could tell."

"Harold, you're kidding, aren't you?"

"No way."

"But Courtney's not like that."

"Oh yeah? How come she only talked to you then?"

"I don't know, did she?"

"Yeah."

"You're all wrong, Harold. After we got into bed, she said you had nice eyes."

"What's that supposed to mean?"

"I'm just telling *you* what she said."

"She say anything else?"

"I can't remember. I was falling asleep by then."

"How come you were talking about me?"

"I don't know, Harold. What do you care?"

"I don't. I just wanted to know."

"Well, I can tell you one thing."

"Yeah?"

"She didn't think you liked her, either."

"Why? I didn't do anything to her."

"You didn't act too hot when you came over."

"You did that jerky introduction number. I didn't know what to say. And besides, you never said she was pretty."

"You think she is?" Janie smiled.

"Yeah, even if she does act like Miss Teenage Beauty."

"You're just as stuck-up sometimes."

"I am not."

"How about when you got your new glasses? We had to stop at every mirror in town."

"That was different."

"And what about the zit you had on your chin last week? You acted worse than your sister."

"Get out!" Harold stood up.

"You did, too." Janie teased. "Hey, I'm getting hungry. Want to make waffles at my house?"

"No, I'm going over to Joel's, but I'll walk you partway back." Harold left his fishing pole leaning against a tree. He and Janie walked single-file through the woods.

An hour later, Janie was settled on the kitchen floor. She was rummaging in her tackle box when Courtney came into the kitchen.

"Morning, Janie."

"Hi." Janie looked up from the snarled fishing line. "Want some juice? It's good; I didn't make it."

Courtney poured for herself. "I never heard you get up, Janie."

"I'm up early. It's the best time to fish."

Courtney sat on the floor next to Janie. "What are you doing?"

"My lures are all mixed up. I was looking for my favorite one."

Courtney sniffed the air. "What's that strange smell?"

Janie rubbed her nose on her arm. "It's pretty bad, isn't it?"

"Did you cook something?"

"Yeah, I had this great idea. I was going to dress up like a nurse and bring you breakfast. But I overcooked the bacon and burned the toast. When I broke the eggs on the counter, I gave up."

"Sounds like a perfect hospital meal to me."

"Yeah, even Fang wouldn't touch it."

"Could I make myself something?"

"You'll be safer."

"Janie, would you want me to teach you how to cook?" Courtney pulled bread out of a plastic bag.

"About as much as you want to fish."

Courtney pressed the toaster oven on. "How do you know I don't want to?"

"You think you would?"

"I could try it. I might like fishing."

"I'd fix up a pole for you and everything."

"Do we have to go through those woods?" Courtney stopped buttering her toast.

"Yeah, but it's daytime, and it's beautiful down near the lake."

"Are there lots of bugs?"

"No."

"What about poison ivy?"

"I'll lend you some jeans and a long-sleeved shirt."

"Okay." Courtney took a bite.

Janie slammed the lid on her green metal box. "Come on, it's getting late already. Bring your breakfast. We have to get out there before nine.

"Why?" Courtney followed Janie back up-stairs.

"Because, after that, the fish have music lessons."

When they were down by the water, Janie began giving instructions. Courtney tried to follow.

"Now, here's the first thing you have to do." Janie took out a small white cup of worms.

Behind them something stirred in the bushes. Courtney turned around. "Did you hear that, Janie? It sounded like a snake."

Janie shrugged and handed Courtney the pole. "Hold this, and I'll do your hook."

Near the trees, a branch snapped. Dead leaves crunched.

"Janie, whatever it is, it's getting closer."

"It's just a raccoon or a skunk."

"A SKUNK!"

"Don't worry." Janie glanced over her shoulder. "It's probably more scared of you."

When they heard the hissing sound, Courtney grabbed Janie's arm. She pointed toward the shrubs.

"I'm telling you, there are no snakes around here. It's a town lake." Janie leaned her pole against the tree, then stood hands on hips, listening.

"Be careful, Janie. It could be poisonous."

"*Hiss. Hiss.*"

Janie threw a stick into the bushes.

"*Hiss. Hiss.*"

"Don't get to close."

Janie kicked a stone into the leaves.

"*Hiss. Hiss.*"

Janie crouched down and stared into the shadowy green darkness. It was the first snake she had ever seen with two blue and two brown eyes.

"Hey, you jerks! What's the big idea?"

Harold and Joel fell back laughing. "Got you, Janie." Harold yelled.

"Not for a second. You guys couldn't scare a flea!" Janie grabbed her pole. "Go fish somewhere else. We were here first."

"*Hiss, hiss, hiss!*" Tall, skinny Joel punched

Harold as they moved onto the rocks upstream. They snorted and whooped as they jumped from one to another.

"I think they're mean." Courtney watched them go.

Janie made a face. "Joel's a creep. Just cause he's older he thinks he knows it all."

"*Hiss, hiss, hiss,*" Joel shouted again.

"Fall in, Joel!" Janie yelled back.

"I don't think they're going to stop, Janie. Do you want to leave?"

"No way! I want you to catch the biggest trout they've ever seen. We'll show them." Janie reached for the line on Courtney's pole.

"Okay?" said Courtney. She turned her attention back to watching Janie.

"You might not like this part, but I'll do it for you." Janie opened the worm cup. She pulled out a fat brown wiggly worm and inspected it.

Courtney gulped as Janie pinched the worm in half with her fingernail. "I'll never be able to . . ."

"There's not much to it." Janie dropped the slimy broken worm into the cup. "You just slide it on like this." Janie's fingers moved carefully around the hook, pushing it through the worm. "And that's all there is to that."

Courtney stared at the worm writhing on the hook. She clamped a hand over her mouth and stood up.

Janie looked at her. "Where are you going?"

Courtney's response was muffled. When she reached the shade of the trees, she called to Janie. "Could we go back soon? I wanted to wash my hair."

Janie slammed down the lid on her tackle box. Though she didn't turn around, she heard laughter. "Wazby . . ." She glared at the water. ". . . sometimes you are so dumb!"

Janie knocked on the bathroom door. "Courtney, can I come in?" She opened the door a crack.

"Hi," Courtney shouted over the hair blower. "I'm done, if you want to get in here."

Janie leaned against the doorframe. "Your hair looks pretty."

"I'm sorry about this morning, Janie. I can't stand the thought of worms, let alone touching them!" Courtney switched off the blower. "Is that dumb?"

"Yeah." Janie smiled as she perched on the sink. "But so what? I can't stand the thought of cooking."

"I knew you wanted me to fish in front of Harold, but . . . those slimy things!"

"That's okay. I feel the same about pots and pans." Janie played with the hole in her sneaker.

"You're not sorry I came?"

Janie looked up. "No way."

"I was really worried."

"Don't be."

"Harold must think I'm such a jerk."

Janie rolled her eyes. "Who knows? I can't figure out what's going on with him. Listen, my mother said I have to start picking berries today. Would you want to help?"

"Sure, Janie."

"It's not much fun."

"At least there's no worms." Courtney giggled.

"Right."

"Let me find my sandals."

"Wear shoes, you'll need them." Janie turned around. "I'll meet you outside in the front."

"I'll be right there." Courtney zipped up her makeup kit.

Janie led Courtney into the front corner of the yard where a high and thick bramble drooped with warm, ripe berries. The air was heavy with insects.

Last summer, when she was learning to walk again, Janie had watched the berries turning slowly from a green to a blackish red. From the porch, she had come to know the habits of every creature who lived beneath the wild blackberry patch. But the birds feasting and their joyful flights with berries in their beaks had caused an ache deep in Janie's heart. Janie tugged at the fruit. "Be careful of the prickers, Courtney. They're killers."

"You know this is the second thing today that I've never done before."

"What was the first?" Janie thrashed around, stomping the tall grass down.

"Fishing, even though I didn't get very far."

"You *never* fished before!" Janie turned around.

Courtney sucked on her reddish purple fingers. "No."

"Where have you been all your life?"

"Doing other things, I guess."

"Yeah, but . . . what else is there?"

"You really like fishing that much? I like this better."

Janie popped a handful of berries in her mouth. "Fishing's the best."

"Better than baseball?"

"Oh sure."

"Then, you know what? I want to try again."

Janie stopped picking. "Fishing?"

"Yes, fishing."

"You don't have to."

"But I really want to."

Janie wiped sticky hands on her jeans. "That's neat. Hey, maybe I could teach you how to fish, and you could show me something."

"Like what?"

"I don't know."

"Janie! I do! I could teach you how to cook."

"And I thought you were my friend. What are you trying to do, kill me?"

Courtney laughed. "It would be fun."

"Maybe for you."

"You like to eat, don't you?"

"Yeah, but what's that got to do with cooking?"

"Oh, come on, Janie!"

"I'd rather live on candy bars."

"Janie," Courtney insisted, "cooking's wonderful. Let me teach you."

Janie made a face. "Nah, I don't think so."

Courtney put one hand on Janie's shoulder. "Do you want to live the rest of your life on food that tastes like the hospital's?"

"No?"

"Well then?"

Janie didn't believe that that was the only food out there, but she knew Courtney really wanted to teach her. "What could we make?"

"You decide."

"How about peanut butter and jelly ice cream?"

"I don't know how to make ice cream, Janie."

"Boy, the one thing . . ."

"Janie! What about jam?"

"What?"

"You said your mother is making it, didn't you?"

"Boy, I don't know about that at all!"

"Think how surprised she'd be."

"Surprised?" Janie threw back her head. "She'd be shocked out of her mind."

"Wouldn't it be worth it, just for that alone?"

"You may have something there."

"We have to find a recipe; that's the only thing."

"We must have a cookbook somewhere in the house."

"You know, my Aunt Vera makes the most wonderful preserves."

"Yeah?"

"If you want, I could call her."

"Okay, but we have to keep this whole thing a secret. I don't want my mother to know."

"But how can we? She'll see us. It takes hours."

"We could do it on Wednesday when she teaches."

"Want me to call my aunt?"

"Yeah." Janie turned toward the bushes. "Pick them berries, kid." She began working furiously.

7

"Okay," said Janie after lunch was over. "My mother just shut her door. We can talk now."

"I think it would be a really good idea if we got everything organized, so all we have to do is make the jam on Wednesday."

"How long will it take? It's really nice out."

"We'll just make sure we have everything."

"Okay, where do we start?"

"I know the berries have to be washed."

Janie ran the cold water. "Think we have enough?"

"Not if you keep eating away."

Janie shoved the bucket under the faucet. "So, I'll leave them alone."

"Do you have jars, Janie?" Courtney looked up from the list she was making.

"I'll go check." She lifted the soaking berries onto the counter.

"And I'll call my aunt. Sure it's safe?"

"Yup, my mother never hears a sound once she's in her darkroom."

Picking up the kitchen phone, Courtney began to dial. "I hope my Aunt Vera is home."

"I'll go find the jars."

"Too bad we can't start right now."

"This is enough kitchen for one day."

Janie headed down to the garage. She was poking around in the cabinets when someone came up the driveway.

Harold squeezed in between the car and the side of the garage. "Hey, can I borrow your mower?"

"Ask my father." Janie didn't turn around.

"What's wrong with you?" He leaned against the red jeep.

Janie went on opening and shutting drawers. "After this morning, what do you think?"

"What's that supposed to mean?"

Janie stood up straight and stared at Harold. She didn't say a word.

"You mean that little joke? That was supposed to be funny. You know HA! HA! HA!"

"It wasn't, Harold."

"Sure, it was. It was a riot."

"Wrong again, Batman!"

"Well, it was Joel's idea, anyway. He wanted to see what Courtney looked like."

"Why didn't you just come over and say hello?"

Harold shrugged. "I don't know."

"If that's how Joel thinks you get a girlfriend, boy, I wouldn't listen to him!"

"Who said anything about a girlfriend?"

"You did, all last week. Why can't you just be decent?"

"Why should I? You said yourself, she doesn't like me, anyway."

"No, I didn't. But if you're trying to get her to hate you, you're doing a terrific job so far!"

"You think she hates me?" Harold cocked his head to one side.

"No, Harold!" Janie roared. "But I wouldn't take any more of Joel's suggestions if I were you."

"Okay, okay," he said looking out the garage door. "Can I borrow the riding mower or not?"

"Hey, listen, we're going fishing tonight. Would you want to come?"

"She's going to fish?"

"Yeah, she really wants to learn."

"Well, maybe I could lend her my extra pole."

"Great."

"I still have to do the grass or I won't be going anywhere tonight."

"You still have to ask. Oh wait, I'll just tell my mother when I go in."

"Thanks." Harold took the keys off the hook near the door. "See you later."

"Right."

It took Janie another fifteen minutes to find the glass jelly jars. She pulled them out from under a basket of rusty garden tools and carried them upstairs into the kitchen.

"Guess what?" Janie dropped the box on the wooden table.

Courtney looked away from the counter where she was writing notes. "What did you say?"

"I just spoke to Harold, and we're all going fishing tonight."

"Oh, Janie!" Courtney dropped the pencil. "I don't know if I want to see Harold after this morning. Couldn't we just fish alone?"

Janie perched on her favorite countertop. "You're not really mad at what he did, are you?"

"No, I just feel so stupid."

"Why?"

"Because of how I acted."

"When I told him you wanted to fish, he was into showing you."

"You're not just saying that, are you?"

Janie looked baffled. "What do you mean?"

"You didn't tell Harold to be nice to me because of what I said last night? About my back?"

"I wouldn't do that."

"I know you're really good friends and . . ."

"Cross my heart."

"Really?"

"Yeah!"

"Okay, I'll go, but I hope tonight isn't awful."

"Just act regular."

"I don't know what regular is, around boys."

"Like when you're with me."

"I never had a boy who was my friend. I never even heard of such a thing."

"It's exactly the same as me and you." Suddenly, Janie laughed and pounded her fist on the counter. "I know what you can do."

"What?"

"Why don't you pretend Harold is a girl?"

"What are you talking about, Janie?"

"I was just thinking if Harold was like a girl to you, then you wouldn't feel so weird around him."

Courtney giggled. "I couldn't."

"Sure you can." Janie laughed. "Why not?"

"But what would I say?"

"Stuff like when you talk to me. Like, 'Hiya Harold, how's it going?'"

Courtney hesitated, but her eyes were sparkling.

"Try it."

"Oh, I can't."

"Come on, just do it."

Courtney stood up tall. "Hiya, Harold . . ."

"Don't stop there; keep talking."

"Hiya, Harold, how's it going?" Courtney tossed her hair back.

"Now something else."

"Like what?"

"What else do you want to say?"

"I don't know. I'm not used to talking to a boy as if he's a girl."

"Janie!" Mrs. Tannenbaum yelled from the second floor.

Janie jumped off the counter. "Quick!" She pointed to the box of jars. "Get rid of that."

"Janie, are you there?" Helene Tannenbaum came halfway down the stairs.

"Yeah?" Janie went to the bottom of the stairwell.

"Is there any coffee left in the warmer?"

"I think so."

"Could you bring it up? I can't leave what I'm doing."

"In a minute." Janie came back to the kitchen counter. Taking a cup down, she said, "Keep practicing. I'll be right down."

Trying not to spill hot coffee on herself, Janie held it with both hands. When she reached her mother's room, she kicked the door open.

Mrs. Tannenbaum reached for the cup. "How's the picking going?"

"Okay, I guess." Janie watched her mother take a sip.

"Is anything wrong?"

"Not really."

"Want to tell me?"

Leaning against her mother's cluttered desk,

Janie said, "It's just harder than I thought it would be."

"Having Courtney visit?"

"It's not just me and Courtney; it's me and Courtney and Harold."

"Oh, I hadn't thought of that."

"She doesn't think he likes her. And he thought she didn't like him."

"That's normal. They both only have you as their friend."

"But they could be great friends." Janie inspected her grubby hands.

"You can't expect two people to automatically like each other just because of you."

"I don't see why not."

"It doesn't work that way, honey."

"Well, it should." Janie bit off a ragged thumbnail.

Mrs. Tannenbaum smiled. "It would be nice."

"Well, I just talked to Harold, and I think he's going to be decent to her. And I told Courtney that, but she's still worried."

"You have to let them decide on their own if they like each other."

"But they're taking *too* long!" Janie flicked the nail scrap into a wastebasket.

"Be a little patient. Don't push them."

Janie made an ugly face. "You always say that."

"It doesn't hurt to try."

"Yeah, it does."

"Where?" Janie's mother mocked gently.

"Right here." Janie pretended to punch herself in the stomach. "And it feels real yucky, too." She headed toward the door.

"That's for sure."

Janie halted in the middle of the room and spun around. "So why are you telling me to . . . ?"

"Because there is no other way."

Janie wasn't sure as she headed down to the kitchen that her mother was right. After all, she thought, the three of them were going fishing tonight, weren't they?

When the doorbell rang that night, Janie and Courtney were straightening up the kitchen. "I'll get that," Janie said. "It's probably Harold."

"Oh, Janie, are you sure?"

"Don't worry, we'll have a great time. Just remember, 'Hiya, Harold.' "

Courtney nodded unconvinced. "I think I'll go comb my hair again."

She rushed upstairs as Janie answered the door. Harold pulled the screen door open, fishing gear in hand.

"What happened to your face?" Janie stepped backwards. "Were you in a fight?"

"No, I nicked myself a little."

"Looks like someone tried to scalp you."

"That always happens when you shave."

"SHAVE!" Janie shouted. "Since when?"

"I've been shaving for years, Janie."

"Is that why you're all full of cuts?"

"Hey, Janie . . ." Harold squinted at her.

"Yeah?"

Just then Courtney came to the front door. She had changed into pale green slacks and a white lacy blouse. "I'm all set, Janie. Hello Harold." She smiled up at him. "How are you?"

"Well, hi." Harold blushed.

Janie rolled her eyes and headed out the door. She led the way over the grass toward the dirt road and then down through the woods.

"Watch your step," Harold was saying to Courtney as they came to the bank. "The moss is slippery."

Courtney chose her footing carefully. When she hesitated before climbing down a small pile of rocks, Harold waited for her.

Near the water, he said, "Janie says you've never fished before?"

"No." She smiled up at him. "But I'd really like to learn."

"It's pretty easy." Harold handed her a pole.

"Will you show me, Harold?"

"Sure thing!" He straightened his shoulders.

While Harold went over the basics of casting out a line, Janie baited the hooks with worm pieces. It was just as well, Janie thought, that Harold was talking to Courtney so she didn't see that part.

The first time Courtney threw the line out, it

caught in the trees and Harold had to yank it free for her. Then she snagged the hook on weeds in shallow water. "I'll never get it," she moaned.

"Keep trying," Harold coaxed. "It just takes practice."

Janie threw her line in the water. She settled cross-legged on the rocks watching Courtney and Harold. They were finally acting decent to one another, Janie thought. Her mother had been wrong.

On the third try, Courtney cast the line into deep water. It was five feet from the shore. "Oh, I did it, Janie! Now what?"

"Just sit and wait."

Courtney settled next to Janie, holding the pole with both hands. "How am I doing?" she leaned over and whispered. "I'm so nervous."

"Super!" Janie reeled in her line.

"So tell me"—Courtney raised her voice—"some more about that magical pasture underwater."

Janie looked out at the lake, which was still high from all the summer rain. "There's this story. One of the stone walls runs into the water where the pasture used to be—"

"Get to the good part, Janie." Harold threw out his own line.

"I am, I am. So anyway, the part of the stone wall that's under water supposedly still has a wooden gate with a cowbell on it."

"That's wonderful, Janie."

"I know it."

"Just think, the bell that once rang for the cows now calls the fish to pasture."

"Hey!" Harold glowed. "That's what I said."

Janie picked a stick with slimy weeds hanging from it out of the water. "If only"—she threw it back—"the city would let all the water drain down in the fall. Then we could get it. I'd love to own a cow bell."

"But Janie, you can't do that. How would the fish find their way?"

"You know, Janie"—Harold came and sat between them—"Courtney's right."

"Well . . ." Janie hedged a bit. ". . . maybe, I wouldn't take it, but I'd love to know if it's really there."

Courtney looked at Harold. "Why do they let the water go down?"

"I'm not sure, but they always do in the fall. You know what the best part is?"

"No, what?" Courtney returned his smile.

"When the lake's really low and there's been warm weather, grass starts to grow all over the field. Then you can believe cows grazed out there once."

"Yeah." Janie nodded. "And the spirit of the great cow roams again."

Over in the west, the sun had dropped behind the trees, thrusting a blazing column of orange across the water's surface. Hidden in the reeds a bullfrog lifted his raspy voice and the peepers continued the song. Harold pulled out his harmonica and began to play a soft melody.

"Oh lovely." Courtney sighed.

And Janie leaned back against a rock. Her friends were finally friends.

8

———————◆———————

Courtney was making her bed the next morning when Janie came into the room. "Want to work on the cooking some more, Janie?"

Janie flopped on her unmade bed. "Wouldn't you rather fish?"

"Not on an empty stomach." Courtney shook out her pillow. "Besides we have to do this lesson for lesson, to keep it even."

"Looks like I can't talk you out of this one, huh?"

Courtney smiled. "You wouldn't do that, would you, Janie?"

"No, not me. Never!" Janie laughed out loud.

"We could do breakfast."

"How about cold cereal?"

"No fair. That's cheating."

"I like waffles. Harold always makes them when I eat at his house."

"Can Harold cook?"

"Yeah."

"He's nice, Janie. I wasn't sure yesterday, but I like him."

"Yup!"

"How old is he?"

"He'll be thirteen next month."

"Does he have a girlfriend?"

"No."

"He seems like he would. He's so good-looking and all."

"You think Harold's handsome?" Janie smothered laughter in her pillow.

"What's so funny?"

Janie uncovered her face. "Nothing really. It's just hard for me to think of him like that. That's all."

"Well, I think he is!"

"Well, maybe he is, I don't know." Janie covered her mouth again with one hand.

"Why doesn't he, Janie?"

"Why doesn't he what?"

"Have a girlfriend?"

"Well, for one thing . . ." She put her hands in her pockets. ". . . his mother won't let him go out on dates." She began pulling out a long strand of knotted fishing line.

"He's not the only one." Courtney stopped adjusting her hair.

"And for another, he doesn't know what you do, to ask a girl out."

"That's a surprise."

"He's been practicing."

"What?" Courtney turned around and faced Janie.

"Yeah, in front of a mirror. He'd kill me for telling you."

Courtney giggled. "You're kidding! What's so hard about asking out a girl?"

"He's worried she might say no to him."

"What girl would say no?"

Janie made a funny face. She pointed an index finger at her chest. "I'll give you three guesses; first two don't count."

"I forgot about that . . . you know what I did once?"

"No! I give up."

"Can you keep a secret?"

"Sure." Janie folded her arms across her chest.

"You promise you won't tell? Not anyone."

"No, I mean, yes." Janie shook her head.

"One time, I practiced kissing a mirror."

"You did?" Janie's mouth dropped. "Why?"

"I wanted to see how I'd look to a boy."

"But a mirror's flat," Janie said, thinking of

all the times she had pressed her face against glass windows.

"I know, and I kept closing my eyes, so I really couldn't tell."

Downstairs the doorbell rang; Fang went crazy barking.

"That's got to be Harold!" Janie jumped off her bed. "Hurry up!"

By the time Janie had run down the hall, Harold had let himself into the house. "Back, Fang! Back!"

"Okay, down, killer!" Janie yelled at the foot of the stairs. Fang rolled over on his back when Janie knelt to pet him. "He wants to be a doberman pinscher when he grows up, Harold. I've been giving him a few pointers."

"Swell," Harold grumbled.

Janie gathered Fang in her arms. "Harold doesn't like you, Fang." The dog growled deep in his tiny throat.

Harold growled back at him.

"Okay," Janie said, "now you two are even. You want to have breakfast with me and Courtney?"

"Are you having anything good?"

"She's teaching me how to cook waffles."

"You!"

"Yeah, me." Janie pivoted around and headed toward the kitchen.

"This I gotta see." Harold followed behind.

Janie stopped short. "Listen, Harold, if you make any more remarks I'm going to have to call this trained killer to finish you off."

"Oh, no! Save me! Save me!" Harold's voice was high and panicky.

"You see, Fang." Janie put the dog on a kitchen chair. "Someone is afraid of you."

Fang whined and wagged his little brown tail. He curled up and shut his eyes.

"Where's Courtney?" Harold said casually.

"She'll be right down. Let's get the stuff out so we're ready."

Harold stretched his arms and yawned. "She's okay."

"Who, Courtney?"

"Who else, Janie?"

"Didn't I tell you?" Janie went to the foot of the stairs. "Courtney are you coming?"

"I'll be right there." Courtney's voice floated down the stairwell.

Janie went back into the kitchen. "How was the fishing this morning?"

"Just a couple of nibbles."

"Maybe this afternoon we could go up to the head of the lake."

"It's supposed to rain." Harold slumped in a chair.

"Aww . . . not again." Janie slammed the refrigerator. "Want some juice?"

"Good morning." Courtney glided into the

kitchen with a load of paperback books in her arms.

"Well, hi." Harold straightened up in his seat. "We thought maybe you'd changed your mind about wanting to teach Janie to cook."

"Oh no. I wanted to show you these."

"What've you got?" Janie crossed the room with a tan plastic pitcher. She could smell Courtney's lilac perfume.

"It's the Greno books. I thought Harold might like them." Courtney put the stack on the table.

"He doesn't go in for fantasy." Janie stood between them. "Listen, I'm going to starve to death. When do we start cooking?"

"I'll look at these later," Harold said. "I have to watch Janie." He pushed the books to one side. "I wouldn't miss this for the world!"

"Fang!" Janie roared. "Get him, Fang!"

Fang raised his head off the chair seat. He wagged his tail, then closed his eyes again.

"No waffles for you, Fang." Janie opened the refrigerator. "Okay, what should I get out?"

"Maple syrup," Courtney said, "milk, eggs."

Harold lifted a large red bowl off the sink. "Where's the box of mix?"

Janie pointed to a top cabinet. "Up there, I think."

"I'll get that stuff." He reached for the stepladder.

"If you have any, Janie, we could make bacon or sausages." Courtney took the items as Harold handed them down.

"I'll see what's here." Janie yanked open one of the refrigerator drawers. "Oh wow, we could have these!"

Courtney leaned over Janie's shoulder. "I think I'm going to be sick."

Janie laughed. "Aren't they cute!"

"You're gross, Janie." Harold watched as she picked the fat brown worms off the lettuce and tomatoes.

"Why do you have them in the refrigerator?" Courtney picked up the bowl and batter mix and moved to the other end of the counter. Harold carried the eggs and milk for her.

"They live longer. Come on, fellas," Janie coaxed, "back into your carton you go. I hope they'll be okay. It's a good thing I found them instead of my mother. She'd have thrown them out."

"They're probably stuffed with lettuce." Harold cracked an egg on the rim of the bowl. "The fish will love them."

"Want some in the batter, Courtney?" Janie wiggled a long skinny worm in midair.

"Not in my batter, you don't," Courtney tried to joke.

Janie tore the brown spots off the lettuce and shut the drawer. The white plastic worm cup went on the top shelf next to the cottage cheese. "What else do we need?"

"Aren't you going to throw out that salad stuff, Janie?" Courtney stopped stirring.

"Nah, what for?"

"Hey, Courtney"—Harold nodded toward the back door—"want to go over to my house and eat? It's just through those trees."

"All of a sudden"—she looked first at Harold then Janie—"I'm not very hungry!"

"You guys aren't any fun, you know that?" Janie slammed the refrigerator door. "Okay, Fang, it's your turn to set the table!"

After they had split the last waffle between themselves and Fang, Harold wiped away his milk moustache. "Now, tell me about this Greno thing."

Courtney folded her napkin. "Once there was a people called the Grens. The books tell how their civilization was destroyed.

"How come?" Harold tilted backwards on his chair. "They got creamed?"

"Well," Courtney began, "it happened during Nimbus's reign."

"Who's he?"

"He was the greatest wizard of all times till he fell into pretending."

"What's that mean?" Harold frowned at Courtney.

"Listen," Janie said, "why don't we do something? Harold's not . . ."

"Wait a minute, Janie. I want to hear about this Nimbus guy."

Janie dropped her head on her arm. She shot some crumbs across the table.

"So what about Nimbus?"

"He didn't listen to what the black sands said."

"Talking sand!" Harold frowned.

"No silly!" Courtney giggled at him "Nimbus had a shell called the royal staircase. He could tell the future with the grains of sand that fell out of it."

"Sounds weird to me." Harold shook his head.

Courtney nodded. "It's better if you read it. I can't make it sound right, telling the story."

"I want to hear more." Harold scratched a pimple on his chin.

"The Grens used to be friends with the Shell Masters, but they had a war."

"Who are they?"

"They were warriors who traded with the Grens. They wore shells and rode into battle on giant snails."

"That sounds neat. So how come there was a war?"

"It had to do with the wizard. I don't want to give it away."

While Janie listened quietly, she scooped sugar out of the bowl and watched the granules fall off the spoon. Finally, she carried her dish to the sink, hoping their conversation would end. But Courtney and Harold had unfolded the map at the front of the book.

Janie wandered into the living room. Outside the rain beat down on the lake. Tree barks were a wet brownish black, the sky a solid steel color. Though there was a greenness all around, it reminded her of winter. Janie shivered.

9

It was raining hard later that same day. Janie sat in front of the television with Courtney and Harold. They were watching an old science fiction film.

"This is so dumb!" Janie squirmed when the commander kissed the woman as the capsule orbited the planet.

"Shush," Harold said. "I've seen this three times. It's great."

"It's so scary." Courtney looked at Janie.

"Well, the guy gets . . ." Janie began.

"Don't tell me, don't tell me." Courtney waved her hands at Janie.

"Fang"—Janie grabbed the dog by the collar—"I love you so, you're everything to me."

"Hey, cut it out, Janie. I'm trying to listen." Harold turned up the sound.

"Come on, Fang." Janie stood up. "Let's blow this popstand."

"Some people . . ." Harold nodded to Courtney.

Janie stomped up the two flights of stairs to her mother's studio. The door was closed, but she banged on it anyway. "Mom, can I come in?"

"Just a second. I have to take the prints out of the fixer."

Janie waited hunched against the wall. Her mother was taking a long time.

"Okay," Mrs. Tannenbaum called. "Come on in."

It was still dark inside when Janie opened the door. Wet photographs hanging from clothespins were strung across the room like laundry. The black and white pictures dripped on the floor.

Janie didn't even notice. She flopped onto the couch. "I don't have anything to do."

"Where's Courtney?" With her hands in her back pockets, Janie's mother stood before the photos, inspecting them.

"She and Harold are watching this goofy love movie, and I don't want to."

"Why don't you find something you want

to do?" She began rolling up the black plastic shades, letting in gray afternoon light.

"Like what? It's pouring out."

"Hey, did I tell you?" Helene Tannenbaum came and sat beside Janie. "John Ransom called. He said the goose—what's his name?"

"Roger."

"Roger's okay. You could go up and see him."

"Mom?" Janie leaned back against her mother. "What were you like when you were a kid?"

"Like you, pretty much."

"You were a tomboy?"

"Sure, I could take on any of my brothers."

"I can't believe that!"

"You just ask Granny what happened when she decided it was time for me to start wearing dresses."

"What did you do?" Janie said still not believing her.

"I ran away from home."

"You did?"

"I spent the night hiding in a cave, near the farm."

"What happened?"

"I got a cold, but I was so proud of myself. None of my brothers had ever done anything like that."

"Was Granny mad?"

"Furious! But my father said it was a good thing for me to have done."

"So what happened? Why'd you change?"

"I started seeing things differently."

"What's that supposed to mean?"

"That I changed."

"But why, why'd you go and change?"

"That's what happens, Janie."

"Didn't you miss it?"

"Being a tomboy?"

"Yeah."

"No, 'cause I didn't stop being one. I just wanted to do other things, too."

"Bet you can't climb trees anymore."

"Who says?" Mrs. Tannenbaum smiled, folding her arms across her plaid shirt.

"I just bet once you stop you lose it all."

"Tell you what, next time we go to Granny's, we'll try out a few of my favorite trees."

"Will you show me the cave? I'd rather see that."

"Sure."

"Can I sleep out there one night?"

"We'll see. It's pretty wild."

"You see, Mom. If you really were still a tomboy, you'd let me." Janie didn't know what to make of the slight smile on her mother's face as they started down the hall.

Janie rang the bell several times. Chimes sounded inside the old Victorian house. Peering through the lace curtains, Janie saw Mrs. Ransom coming down the long, dark hall. When the silver-haired woman opened the door, Janie smelled something baking.

"Hello, hello, Janie Tannenbaum!" She wiped her pudgy hands on a red print apron.

"Hi. I came over to see Roger. My mother told me Mr. Ransom called." Janie watched the pink mole above the woman's lip move when she smiled.

"Well now, that crazy goose isn't home yet. It'll be a few more days."

"Oh, I thought he was back."

"No, but it was sweet of you to come by. Mr. R.'s been so worried about him."

"Well, say hello to Roger for me." Janie took a step backwards on the wooden porch, suddenly feeling a little silly.

"Why don't you go to the barn. Mr. R. will be glad to see you."

"You sure it's okay?"

"Yes, of course."

Janie wandered down around the side of the old white house with its crumbling decoration and peeling paint. From the rise in the muddy driveway, she could see that the meadow was empty. Even the pond where the ducks and geese clustered was deserted.

She eased herself through the slightly open barn door. Inside, it was dim and smelled of hay and manure. Along with the buzzing flies and grunting pigs, Janie heard a deep voice. She drew closer and listened.

"Once in a dark and lonely corner of the world lived a woman who loved trees. Everyday she would journey out . . ."

Suddenly a large cow's head thrust itself over the stall, startling Janie. She jumped back, and the cow shook its head sideways.

"Easy girl," the voice coaxed. "Hello, who's there?"

Janie moved around the huge head and up to the open stall gate. "Hello, Mr. Ransom. I just stopped by to see Roger, but your wife said . . ."

"Come in, come in." He leaned over and pulled up a red plastic crate for Janie. When she hesitated, he asked, "Not afraid, are you?"

"No." Janie shook her head. "I just wanted to say I'm sorry about that day . . ."

"Say no more; it was a bad day." He patted the crate. "I'm glad for the company."

Janie sat down. She had never been inside a cow stall before.

Mr. Ransom went back to milking. "This here is Lady Fern."

Janie listened to the steady rhythmic blasts of milk hitting the inside of the large silver pail. She watched the cow's enormous black and white flanks breathing in and out and the almost delicate legs that supported her massive weight.

"Fern here will stand still for a good story, but she likes poetry the best."

"Is that what you were doing when I came in?"

"Yep, it's the only way she'll be milked."

"That's pretty neat. What kinds of stories does she like?"

"Ever hear of *The Rhyme of the Ancient Mariner*?"

"I don't think so."

"It's about an old man who's been to sea. She likes that, also *Gulliver's Travels*. Stories about different places."

"That's amazing."

"Now you take Zelda, over there. She's nothing but an old stay-at-home gossip. She likes to know everyone's problems."

Janie looked over her shoulder at the light brown cow, chewing straw. "No kidding."

"She don't hold still for no stories or poetry, couldn't care less, just gossip and troubles. The worse they are, the better she likes it."

Janie laughed. "I didn't know that about cows."

"Yep, each one has her own personality. You hang around them enough, you'll see it. Do you like animals?"

Janie nodded. "Yeah."

"I could tell. Actually, it wasn't me that knew, but Fern."

Janie looked at the spotted head she was sitting under. "What do you mean?"

"Fern's skittish with people around her. But

she must like you, otherwise she'd have kicked over her pail by now."

"I think you're swell too, Fern." Janie stroked the cow's side gently.

"Out in the bin, there's turnips. You can give her one."

"Cows eat turnips!"

"Just try her."

"Doesn't it make the milk taste funny?"

"It's just for me and the Mrs., and we like our milk tangy."

Janie found the biggest turnip in the storage bin. Then carefully she extended a hand to Fern. The cow eyed her blankly but accepted it. The wet pink tongue felt like sandpaper when it brushed over Janie's hand. Fern crunched away noisily.

"Great sound." Janie sat down again. Fern and Mr. Ransom and everything about the barn had a sweet-and-sour milk smell. Janie hunched over watching the old man's gnarled hands milking.

"Ever try to milk a cow?"

"No, but I'd like to."

"You have to know some poetry."

Janie scratched her head. "I don't really, but I'll learn just so I can try."

Mr. Ransom looked up from his milking. His eyes twinkled. "Tell you what. Next time you come over, you can learn to milk."

"Great." Janie watched as he carefully moved

the pails to one side. Next he washed off the pink udder with a damp cloth. "Why'd you do that?"

"Prevents disease. Well, she's done." He stood up slowly, bracing his back with one hand.

Janie got up also. "Can I watch you milk Zelda?"

"She's dried off for now."

"Does that mean no milk?"

"Yep," she'll be calving soon." He stooped over and lifted the pails, one in each hand.

"Oh wow! When?"

"A week or so."

"Could I watch?" Janie followed him out of the stall.

"It usually happens in the middle of the night. Cows are real private creatures, especially Ms. Zelda."

"For someone who's so nosy, that's not fair."

Mr. Ransom chuckled, and Janie waited while he checked the latch on the back door. She leaned on a burlap bag filled with chicken feed and fingered the pitchfork hanging from a rusty nail.

"You're a pretty smart little gal," he said coming back into the main part of the barn.

Janie beamed. "Want me to help carry a pail?"

"No, but how about you get the lights?"

"Okay."

"Leave the one in the cow stalls on." Mr. Ransom shuffled out.

Janie waited while he closed the wooden doors behind them. "This is sure a neat place."

"You think so, do you?"

"Yeah, I like barns a lot. Sometimes I hang out in that old one, you know where the lake is?"

"Well, now, that was my old granddaddy's place." He moved slowly across the road.

"How come it's deserted over there?"

"No one wants to live on a farm, these days." He stopped in the middle of the yard and put down the pails. "All this land"—his stubby finger pointed to the field—"down to the main road where the bus goes used to be green pasture land."

For an instant Janie had a glimmer of what it must have been like with no houses around, not even her own, just cows roaming inside stone walls. "What happened?"

"It's hard work, tilling dirt and caring for animals. My brother, even my kids, didn't want it; we sold the land."

"But what'll happen . . . ?" She didn't want to say when you die. "What will happen to Fern and Zelda?"

Mr. Ransom picked up the two nearly full milk pails. "I hope something good. Well, stop by again. Fern'll teach you how to milk."

"Fern?" asked Janie still thinking about the land.

"And brush up on your poetry. Fern's also partial to Shakespeare," he called over his shoulder as he went around the side of the house.

Janie started for the metal gate. It wasn't till she was halfway down the road and could see her house through the trees that she remembered Courtney and Harold watching television.

10

It was getting on toward sunset when Harold said to Courtney, "Want to take a walk?" He was leaning on the porch railing after supper.

She smiled. "I'd love to."

Janie jumped off the picnic table and headed for the steps. She was determined to lead the way, but the slowness of Courtney's and Harold's pace made her turn around. "Where are we going?" she yelled.

Harold stopped speaking to Courtney. "Up to the wall. I wanted to show it to Courtney."

Janie bolted through the woods, then realized she was way ahead of them again. She sat on a damp rock and waited. A family of ants carrying a blackberry down the path took her attention. She cleared leaves out of their way and watched till they disappeared into a sandy pit.

A chipmunk ran across the roots of a tree and stopped short when he spotted her. The little tan-and-white striped body scolded her for being in his way.

"*Che-che-chee.*" She talked back. He took a different route to his hole.

Janie heard Courtney and Harold coming up the path. He was talking about music.

"All I really want to do is play the harmonica."

"Why don't you?"

"My mother wants me to be a violinist like her father."

Courtney pulled a leaf from a tree and twirled it around by the stem. "Did you ever tell her?"

"It's no use," Harold grumbled as they came upon Janie.

"Gee, you guys!" She stood up. "It'll be winter before we get there."

"Lead on," Harold said to Janie.

But Janie waited and walked with them. No one was speaking as they came to the stone wall, which tumbled into the water and disappeared. In a place where the rocks were not overgrown with moss, Janie climbed the wall and walked down to the water's edge. She was expecting Harold to follow. He sat on the ground beside Courtney.

Slowly Janie walked back past her friends. She climbed into a big tree that had grown against the stones. "Harold and I have a contest to see who can get to the bell—"

"We told her already."

"Oh yeah," Janie said softly, "I forgot." In the gathering darkness of her green hiding place, Janie looked down at her hands. Her fingernails were chipped, and there was dirt under them. In her left palm was a small scar.

"Tomorrow," Harold was saying to Courtney, "I could take you to this spot where the deer live. We might even see them since the summer's almost over."

"Hey you two!" Janie began climbing down. "Want to go dig up worms? The ground's real soft."

Harold turned to Courtney. "Would you like to? They're all at the top after it rains."

Courtney smiled nervously. "I don't know if I can handle that. I think I'd just rather stay here."

Janie turned away. "I'll see you at home." She ran quietly through the woods ignoring the stinging tears that fell across her face.

Janie heard the front door slam. Quickly, she slipped into bed and tried to look fast asleep as Courtney came into the room. Even when Courtney shook her arm, Janie just moaned and rolled over. But then, after Courtney climbed into bed, Janie lay awake listening to her breathing for a very long time.

The next Janie knew, she was listening to the raspy breath of something close to her. And when she turned around, the giant glass bird was after her again. Janie ran and ran, harder, faster. But always he was there catching up, coming closer, his flat bill reaching out to kiss her. "I'll get you yet, I'll get you. Little girl, little girl, little girl," he cried out.

Janie went rushing into darkness, till she smashed into an invisible barrier. Trapped, she beat her fists against it. Then slowly, very slowly, Janie awoke from the dream, with her hands against the bedroom wall.

For what seemed like a long time, Janie lay there panting. "It was a dream, just a dumb dream," she told herself over and over again until she really believed she was awake. Slowly Janie sat up. The figure in the other bed was a lump in the darkness.

Janie stumbled down the hall looking for her mother. She found her curled up in bed, reading. Janie stood in the doorway, rubbing her eyes against the lights.

"Janie!" Mrs. Tannenbaum looked up. "Are you all right?"

Janie squinted, coming across the room. "I had that dream again."

"Come crawl in bed."

Janie moaned, flopping down on her father's side. "Where's Daddy?"

"Working late at the studio." Helene Tannenbaum pulled the covers up around Janie. "What's wrong, honey? Courtney and Harold still?"

"Yeah, I guess."

"What's going on?"

"Now, they're starting to act like boyfriend and girlfriend."

"Oh, Janie! I didn't know. Are they excluding you?"

"No, but I feel like a dumb little kid with them."

Helene Tannenbaum put her arm around Janie. "This kind of thing happens when you grow up. It's awful."

"It's yucky; I hate it."

"When I was thirteen, I used to think I was going to die. I'd lie in bed and think about what kind of flowers I wanted on my coffin when things were really bad."

In spite of herself, Janie laughed.

"Once I even picked out what I wanted to wear in the casket."

"What happened to you?"

"Same thing. My best friend and a boy I liked."

"Yeah, but Mom, this is Courtney. Me and Courtney. It's not supposed to happen with her."

"Oh, Janie, I know, but it does sometimes."

"I can't believe it."

"I know; I couldn't either. I told my mother to bury me in my new bib overalls."

For a long time Janie sat with her fingers pressed against her face. It was all so confusing, she didn't know what to think. "Mom, do you think there's something wrong with me?"

Mrs. Tannenbaum frowned. "What do you mean wrong with you?"

"All of a sudden everyone I know wants to do junk like go out on dates. Maybe I'm retarded or something?"

"You know better than that, Janie."

"I was thinking maybe something happened to my brain when I had that operation."

"I think you're just interested in other things, that's all."

"Like what?"

Mrs. Tannenbaum laughed. "That I don't know."

Janie sighed. "I don't either." She snuggled up next to her mother's side. The pillow beneath her head smelled like her father.

"Mind if I leave the light on? I want to finish this article?"

"Nope." While listening to the soft sound of her mother turning pages, Janie drifted off to sleep. The red bird didn't bother her again.

11

Janie drifted up from sleep to the sound of
the owl's sad, sad voice. She was in her own
bed and vaguely recalled her father's kiss when
he'd carried her back during the night.

Rolling over, Janie found she was alone. The
other bed had been neatly made. It must be
almost noon, Janie thought. Blocks of sunlight
were already touching the middle of her rug.

The phone rang. Half-dressed, Janie rushed
into her mother's room. "Hello?"

"Hi, honey. Did I wake you?" Mrs. Tannenbaum's voice sounded concerned.

"No, I was up. Where are you?"

"At school. Today's my class, remember?"

"Oh yeah."

"I gave them a break. I wanted to see if you were okay."

"I'm all right." Janie recalled last night's dream.

"I told Courtney not to wake you. I thought you needed to catch up on sleep."

"Thanks," said Janie, quietly.

"Think you'll be okay till I get home?"

"Yeah. When will you be back?"

"About three. Call Mrs. Wazby if you have a problem."

"I know."

"That's my girl; I'd better run now."

"Bye, Mom. See you later." After she had put down the receiver, Janie didn't move off her mother's bed. Today was the day she and Courtney were supposed to do the jam.

Janie scratched a mosquito bite buried under her thick hair. Maybe while they were cooking, she could explain to Courtney all the crazy things she was feeling. Like how she wanted her two friends to like each other but not as boyfriend and girlfriend. That it felt super gross to be left out.

Janie looked at herself in the antique mirror hanging on the bedroom wall. It wasn't really fair, she tried to tell herself, that she didn't want Harold as a boyfriend and didn't want him to date Courtney either. And when she asked herself why, there was a cold black space inside her, which offered no answers.

In confusion, Janie went back to her room to dress. Somehow she had to figure out a way to tell Courtney so they could still be friends.

"Courtney?" Janie called going downstairs. There was no answer from the living room. She stuck her head in the kitchen. Deserted.

Janie stepped onto the porch. The day was beautiful, clear and sunny. "Court-NEY." Janie yelled across the yard. Only the crickets, making music for a hot day, replied. "COURT-ney." She tried once more, before letting the screen door slam.

There was no one in the family room, either. Janie took the berry buckets out of the downstairs refrigerator. She left them on the stairs. In the garage, she collected the jar lids. At least she'd have the junk ready when Courtney showed up. Then they could talk.

On the second trip to the kitchen, something made Janie remember Harold's invitation to Courtney. They had gone off earlier this morning to see the deer. There would be no jam today.

"Rats!" Janie stomped into the kitchen. "I hope you have a million zits on your nose, Harold Wazby. She dumped everything on the counter.

"And I hope you fall in the swamp, Courtney." Janie ran out.

She dashed down the porch steps and around the side of the house, then cut through a neighbor's back yard and onto the road. Only when she reached the top of the hill did she think about where she was going.

Her breath was coming heavily when she climbed the stone wall that surrounded Ransoms' pasture. Janie stopped running when she saw Fern and Zelda standing in the shade of the trees. She made herself walk slowly the rest of the way.

Both cows were nibbling grass as Janie approached. Fern picked her head up halfway, but eyed Janie indifferently.

"Zelda?" Janie sat on a large boulder near the trees.

The brown cow's tail flicked flies off her back legs. She went on chewing.

"Listen, Zelda," Janie began. "I'm having a problem. You think you could give me some advice?"

Zelda stopped chewing her cud.

Janie spent the entire afternoon watching the cows. When the sun began to sink, she followed Fern and Zelda across the pasture, over the rise and back toward the barn. Near the muddy entrance, they waited patiently to be let in.

"Well, look who's here." Mr. Ransom swung open the wooden door. He smiled. "Learn any good poetry yet?" The cows plodded inside.

Following behind, Janie shook her head. "No, but I want to try milking."

Mr. Ransom nodded. "Fill the bucket with warm water." He motioned toward the spigot. "I'll get the hay."

Janie watched him climb the handmade ladder up to the loft. She could hear him grunting as he pitched the huge bales of hay over the side. When they hit the floor, they sent up a great cloud of dust.

Sneezing, Janie filled the pail with water. She was pulling two crates close to Fern's rear legs when Mr. Ransom returned. "Good girl." He lowered himself with a groan.

Janie watched as he dipped a rag in the water. "The udders," he said, "need cleaning before you milk. You never know what they've been sitting in." Very gently, he washed the dirt away.

His fat stubby hands stroked the distended udder. He placed two fingers around each teat and began to pull first one then the other down gently. Before long he was making two even jets hit the bottom of the pail. "Want to try now?"

"You think she'll let me?"

"You know what we'll do; let's fool her. I'll tell her a story while you milk."

Janie switched places with the old man. She rested her head against the cow's flank as she'd seen him do. Then very slowly, gingerly even,

Janie put her thumb and index finger around the cow's teat. She waited to see what Fern would do.

"Now very carefully," Mr. Ransom said, "pull down on her as if you were stripping air out of a skinny balloon."

At first the milk squirting out came in uneven blasts, but pretty soon Janie was using both hands in time. "I can't get as much milk as you." She stopped for a moment.

"Let's see your hands." He held out his.

Janie put her hands in Mr. Ransom's. Next to his, her hands seemed fragile.

"You have perfect hands," he said. "They're small enough to get around her littlest teat. When Fern first started milking, my wife had to do her because my hands were too fat. I couldn't get the little ones."

"Really?"

Mr. Ransom pressed Janie's hands inside his own. "All you need is a little practice."

Janie swung around again. "Okay."

"They may even ache some in the beginning, but that's because you're strengthening muscles."

Janie shut her eyes and concentrated on the milking. Fern had such a wonderful smell, like sour milk only not real sour. All around her the barn was still except for the droning of flies and piglet squeals.

Mr. Ransom got up and walked away. Janie

thought he was leaving, but in a moment he returned with a beaten-up blue book.

"This is her favorite of the stories." He opened to the beginning page and cleared his throat. "It was the best of times, it was the worst of times . . ."

With her eyes closed, Janie let the words of the olden story and Mr. Ransom's singsong voice carry her away.

Janie hesitated outside her closed bedroom door. She hadn't said a word to Courtney all through dinner, and she wasn't sure she wanted to now. But she needed her shoes. Janie shoved open the door.

Propped up with pillows, Courtney was painting her nails. "Janie, where were you all day? No one could find you."

"I had to talk to a cow." Janie opened her closet and reached for her gray and pink sneakers.

"You talked to a cow?" Courtney giggled.

"What's so funny about that?"

"Nothing, I guess. I just wish you had come down to the lake."

"What for?"

"Harold made a picnic lunch. And he showed me how to do the dead-man's float. Janie, I'm really learning to swim."

The cold black space in Janie's heart flapped open. "I thought I was going to teach you!"

Courtney looked up from her hands. "You seem really upset, Janie. Are you angry?"

Janie crossed her arms over her chest. Within her, the black space stretched itself into a long dark tunnel.

"Janie, what's wrong? You've been acting so strange?"

"Me!" Janie shouted. "All of a sudden the only thing you care about is getting a boyfriend!" Janie flopped down on her bed.

"Janie, no!"

"Oh, yeah!" She began tying her sneakers.

"I thought you wanted me and Harold to be friends."

"What about the jam? We were supposed to do that today." Janie stood up.

"Oh, Janie! I forgot."

Janie backed out of the room. "Some friend . . ."

"Janie, wait! Come back. You don't understand."

But Janie didn't wait. She disappeared into the deepening twilight, running away from listening, trying to escape what she did not want to know.

Only when the fireflies speckled the darkness with their bits of light did Janie trek back through the old apple orchard. Halfway through the overgrown field, she stopped short. Then, watching her footing, she crept along the stone wall approaching the water. A breeze coming in off the lake fanned her flushed skin. She forced herself to wait till she was completely calm.

"On guard!" She shouted their old signal and leaped over the wall.

Harold had only a second to drop his pole before Janie jumped him. "Are you crazy!" He tried to ward off her fists. "Cut it out, Janie!"

"No way, you creep." Janie lunged for his chest. "Thanks," she panted, "for leaving me." Together they tumbled down the mossy bank.

"What are you talking about?" He pinned Janie's legs by sitting on them. "We left you a note."

"What note?"

"On the pegboard, near the phone."

As if someone had stuck a pin into a balloon, Janie lay still. Harold rolled off her but was ready for another attack.

"Wrestle with me, Harold," Janie said, unable to move. "Like we used to."

"No."

"Why not?"

Harold didn't answer.

Janie drew up her legs. Resting her head on her knees, she said, "You let me win that fight when I got home from the hospital, didn't you?"

Even in the dark she could see his face flush. He couldn't look at her. "I got scared."

"Scared! Scared of what?"

"That I could hurt you."

"You know how creepy that felt."

"I didn't think of that."

"You think I'm some kind of weakling since my operation?"

"It's got nothing to do with that."

"Oh, yeah? Then why won't you ever fight with me? Or do any of the other stuff we always did?"

"It's no fun anymore."

"Sure it is."

"You know it all! Right, Janie?" Harold stood up.

"What are you talking about?"

"It's not fun *for me.* All you want to do is show-off, prove you're smarter and tougher than . . . the whole world."

"That's not true!" Janie looked up at Harold.

"And if somebody tries to be decent or kind, you go nuts."

"I do that?" Janie said, dismayed. She watched Harold turn around.

"It's just not fun like it used to be, Janie." He disappeared into the darkness.

12

Later, she kept going over and over the fight with Harold. Each time made her more confused.

In the other bed, Courtney was fast asleep. When Janie had first come into the darkened room, she thought Courtney was faking it. But her sleep was real now, Janie was certain.

Janie listened to her own shallow breathing, also heard her parents come upstairs and close their bedroom door. A pang of loneliness swept over Janie. Even though it was a crazy idea, she felt like the whole world was sleeping and she was the only one wide awake. And not only was she alone, she had no friends left.

Janie lay awake a long time with her jumbled thoughts, trying to decide what she should do, then trying not to figure it out. To make herself fall asleep, she punched up her pillow then flipped it over to the cool side. She counted backwards, from one hundred down to one. She took deep breaths and let them out slowly.

Then she gave up. Fumbling in the dark, Janie gathered her sneakers and shorts. She dressed in the hall and tiptoed downstairs.

Outside, the moon shone on the front lawn, making it almost as bright as day. Janie sat on the front stoop, listening to the trees sighing in the breeze, listening to a great bullfrog croaking down on the banks of the lake. In the woods, something rustled in the leaves. A raccoon or opossum, she thought. Janie had never been out in the middle of the night, at least not alone like this. It was wonderful, she decided, and exciting.

"Just a quick walk," she told herself, heading down the driveway. But when she reached the road, Janie turned up the hill. She ran all the way to the barn. The old door creaked when she pulled it back. Inside, one bare bulb was lit.

"Evening, Fern." Janie stepped up to the stalls.

"How goes it, Zelda?" She scratched the cow's underchin.

Just to see the view, Janie climbed the ladder

into the loft. A streak of moonlight shone through the window. She stretched out on a bale of hay. Then slowly, slowly, so slowly that she didn't even realize it, Janie fell sound asleep.

In her dreams, though, someone was screaming in pain. She wanted to help, but didn't know what to do. Finally, she awoke with a start. The noise was coming from down below.

Climbing down, Janie heard the cows shifting about. With her head stretched out, Zelda was bellowing long, heavy moos.

"What's the matter, girl? What's wrong?" Janie tried to stroke her, but the cow's head reared away, her eyes wide. She bellowed again.

"Hang on, cow. I'll get someone."

Janie ran across the moonlit yard. She banged on the door with her first and groped for the bell with her other hand. "Mr. Ransom, wake up, wake up!" she shouted. "There's something wrong with Zelda."

Janie waited and waited. When the light went on inside, Mr. Ransom, in a long blue bathrobe, opened the door.

"What's the matter, child?"

"It's Zelda. I think she's having . . . having . . ."

"Now, calm down. Just calm down." The white-haired man opened the door wide.

"I think Zelda's having her baby, but something's wrong."

Just then another great bellow came out of the barn. Casting his eyes there, Mr. Ransom stood absolutely still.

"You see? She sounds like she's dying."

"Come in. I have to get dressed." Halfway up the stairs, he turned around. "Janie, do your folks know you're out?"

Janie shook her head. She had completely forgotten the time.

"Give them a call."

Outside there was another bellow. Both stared out the open door.

"Couldn't I wait till later?"

Mr. Ransom's voice boomed out from the top floor. "Do it now, Janie."

Obediently, Janie went to the old black phone on the corner table. While she dialed, Mr. Ransome came down in heavy boots and bib overalls.

The phone rang three times before she heard her father's sleepy voice saying, "Hello?"

"Dad, it's me."

"Janie, where are you?"

"I'm up at Ransoms'."

"Are you all right?"

"Yes, but Zelda's not, I don't think She's having a baby. I want to stay and help. Can I?"

"Janie, how long have you been out of the house?"

"I don't know. Not too long."

Janie could hear her parents talking. She had

no idea what they would say. "Yes," came the answer when she was about to give up.

"Janie." It was her mother's voice.

"Yeah?"

"Don't get in the way, and be very quiet. Cows don't like it if—"

"Mom," Janie interrupted, "have you ever seen a cow give birth?"

"Yes," Mrs. Tannenbaum said as if thinking the same thoughts as Janie. "And I want to see it again. I'm on my way." She hung up the phone.

Janie found Mr. Ransom pitching hay into a large square room next to the stalls. He had moved Zelda there. The cow was standing quietly facing the corner.

"Is she okay?" Janie whispered.

"She's in labor."

"Do cows always bawl like that?"

"Yes, some. She may be a little scared. She had a hard time with her first calf."

"Can I help?"

"No. She knows what to do."

"Is the vet coming, too?"

"Only if a problem develops. Otherwise Zelda will figure it out for herself. Why don't you sit over there so she doesn't get nervous."

Janie settled outside the door where the cow couldn't see her. Mr. Ransom sat on a bale of hay just inside the door.

"How long?" Janie whispered.

"We just wait."

"Hello." Mrs. Tannenbaum knelt beside Janie. "Is everything okay?"

"Fine." Mr. Ransom nodded. "Good to see you."

The three of them were quiet then. Each watched Zelda, thinking private thoughts. Outside the wind rocked in the trees, and the night watched the moon roll across the sky.

Zelda was quiet too, as if she were resting. Then the bellowing started again. What looked like water tinged with blood rolled down the cow's back leg and dripped onto the hay.

"Look Janie," her mother said, "under the tail."

At first all Janie could see were the muscles flexing. Then in the opening under Zelda's tail the tip of something dark appeared but was sucked back in again. It emerged again, a little more, then slid away.

The third time the dark thing emerged, and she knew it was the calf's toes. Quite suddenly there were legs, two real living legs thrust out of the cow. It made Janie shudder.

When the nose appeared, Janie held her breath. The head was still within a hazy sack, which looked like a blue plastic bag. "Is the calf dead?"

"I don't think so." Mr. Ransom crept across

the room and stood behind Zelda. As the calf's legs and head dropped toward the floor, he gently eased the newborn into the hay.

The cord connecting the baby to its mother snapped. Janie watched as Mr. Ransom dipped the end on the calf into something brownish orange. "I'll need some help with this, Helene."

Together they carried the calf toward the stall in the other corner. It took the three of them to lift it over the railing so the head hung down.

"Why?" Janie stepped back.

"To make sure her lungs are cleaned out of fluid."

The calf remained quiet and motionless. When it sneezed, a long gob of mucus dripped to the floor.

Mr. Ransom placed the calf in the straw beside Zelda. She licked away the remaining mucus.

Only then did Janie take her first deep breath, as if she'd been holding it the whole time. Looking down at the tan calf with the white spots on its side, Janie held onto her tears. It had been so painful, but there Zelda was cleaning up her new baby.

Already the little calf seemed to be coming out of a fog, trying to figure out what to do with its four wobbly legs. Each one wanted to go in a different direction. She staggered up, then fell over.

"Can't we help?" Janie whispered.

"She'll find her mother soon." Mrs. Tannenbaum put her arm around Janie's shoulder. "And then she'll start nursing."

Moments later, the calf began to suckle. Warm milk dribbled down the baby's chin.

"I can't believe it's all over." Janie looked up at her mother.

"Just beginning." Mr. Ransom leaned on a pitchfork. "Why don't you come back later? They'll be out in the pasture."

"Okay." Janie and her mother started for the barn door.

"Janie?" Mr. Ransom called after her.

"Yeah?" Janie turned around and went back inside.

"Think of a good name."

"Really?" Janie's hands went to her hips. "Can I?"

"Yes. You were the first one here. You get to name her."

The dawn sky was streaked with pinks and blues. The wind whispered in the apple grove, and there was a thin frost on the meadow grass.

"Mom?" Janie looked around not seeing her mother. "Where are you?"

"Here," came the answer, without saying where.

"Mom," Janie shouted again.

"Yes, over here."

Janie followed the sound of her mother's laughter. "Mom, I can't find you." Janie stopped in the grove.

"Up here, silly."

Janie looked up into the tree heavy with green apples. "What are you doing?" She began to climb. Her mother was standing on the first limb.

"It's such a good morning for being born. I wanted to see the view."

Janie perched on a branch above her mother's shoulder. "I get to name the calf. Know any good names?"

"We used to call them Francine, Roberta, Lily."

Janie made a face. "Those are terrible. They're for old lady cows."

"You'll think of something."

"Mom, did you mind having a baby?"

Mrs. Tannenbaum looked away from the lake. "What do you mean?"

"Did it hurt? Zelda bled a lot."

Mrs. Tannenbaum leaned against the trunk. "It hurt some, but not impossible. And when I saw you . . . I thought about how you were a part of me and yet not part of me." She looked at Janie. "It's hard to talk about. Nothing I can say would tell you how it really was."

"You think I could be a good mother?"

"Sure, if you want to be."

Janie leaned her head against the trunk. "When I was five, I thought I'd be lousy. I forgot to feed my dolls for whole weeks at a time."

"I wouldn't worry about that. You always reminded us."

"Did I?"

"Ask your father."

Janie took a deep breath. She plucked an apple from the tree and began rubbing it against her jeans.

"Come on." Mrs. Tannenbaum began to climb down. "Your father will think we both ran away from home. Let's go."

13

But Janie didn't go home with her mother. There was something else she had to do. She rang the bell at Harold's house, but no one answered. Giving up, she tramped down through the woods.

She jumped the stream and stopped on the moss-covered bank. There was Harold sitting on his usual rock, which jutted into the lake. Seeing him from behind, Janie suddenly didn't feel so sure of herself. She moved partway down the rocky bank.

"Hey," she yelled. "Harold!"

He turned and shouted back. "What do you want?"

Janie didn't move. "I just wanted to tell you I watched a calf being born this morning."

"At Ransoms'?" He seemed interested.

"Yeah, it was neat."

"I saw one, too."

"Isn't it great?"

They were shouting back and forth at one another, and all of a sudden it seemed silly. Janie started down the path. "We probably woke up everyone all the way around the lake."

"Maybe not everyone." He watched her sit on a rock. "Who calved?"

"Zelda. Who'd you see?"

"Fern. I had to do a report. Mr. R. let me watch the spring . . . you were away."

Janie had the feeling she and Harold could go on and on about cows, with neither of them bringing up what they were really thinking. "Harold, listen, I found the note when I went home last night."

"So I was right."

"Yeah, you were. Sorry about that." She didn't want to sound flip. "I really mean it."

"It's okay. I knew you were upset."

"I sure was."

"I'm glad it happened."

Janie frowned at him. "Huh?"

"Well, I wanted to talk about that day, but I couldn't just walk up to you and say, 'Ahh, Janie, about that fight . . .'"

"How come?"

"It was too hard or something, I don't know."

"I guess I haven't wanted to either. It took Courtney coming here to . . . Courtney!" Janie remembered last night. "Listen, Harold, I have to go talk to her. Come over later. Okay?"

"Right."

"See you." Janie ran into the woods.

For the second time, Janie closed the door to her own room. Courtney was still sound asleep. Janie crossed the hall to her parents' room.

"Daddy." She sat on the edge of the bed.

"Hmmm . . . ?" Her father rolled over.

Janie shook his shoulder. "Wake up. It's time, Mommy said."

Mr. Tannenbaum pulled the sheets over his head. "I'm not going in today."

"Mommy says you have to get up anyway."

He groaned again but made no movement. Janie lifted up the sheet.

"Dad, do you remember all those times you woke me up for school by sprinkling water on my face?"

Janie's father opened one eye; it stared at her. "You wouldn't!"

She smiled. "I might even flash the radio on and off a few times."

Mr. Tannenbaum pushed himself up almost into a sitting position. "No rest for the wicked." He yawned.

Janie handed him a mug of coffee. "Mommy said this would help."

"Bless you." He closed his eyes when he drank the first mouthful.

Janie's father's hair was tousled, his eyes bleary from lack of sleep. The curly black hair on his chest had a few white ones scattered through it.

"Seeing the calf born was great. You should have been there to film it."

"I'm not so sure the cow would have appreciated the flood lights. By the way, miss . . ."

"Yeah?" Janie knew what was coming.

"About your disappearing out of the house in the middle of the night."

"I know."

"No more of that."

"Okay, but I'd never have seen the calf, if I—"

"Janie. Did you hear me?"

"Yes."

"Running up and down country roads in the dark is dangerous."

"I know but—"

"Janie, we'd have let you go, if you asked."

"Everyone was asleep."

"Janie—" He put the mug on the nightstand. "We need to know where you are at all times."

"What about if I'm grown up and I'm working for the FBI on a secret mission? Do I have to call home then?"

"No." Mr. Tannenbaum rumpled her hair. "When you're older, it won't be as important. With my crazy job, I always let your mother know."

"Okay, but I'm not going to be a spy, anyway?"

"Really? What is it this week?"

"I either want to be a farmer or a vet."

Mr. Tannenbaum threw back the covers. "One calf does not a vet make."

"Huh?" said Janie.

"That's the worst yet." Mrs. Tannenbaum stood in the doorway. "Come on, breakfast is ready. We've got a busy day ahead of us."

"My daughter wakes me up in the middle of the night, and my wife hates my jokes. How I suffer!" He emptied his mug of coffee.

"You think that's bad. I cooked breakfast so you have to clean the kitchen." She was gone by the time the pillow hit the wall.

Janie knocked on the door before entering her own bedroom. "Courtney?" Janie called softly. "Are you awake? Can I come in?"

Courtney was leaning over her half-packed suitcase. Her eyes were red and puffy when she turned to face Janie. She opened her mouth to say something then stopped herself.

Janie flopped on her bed exhausted. She really wanted to close her eyes and sleep for a while.

"Janie, please, listen to me." Courtney sat beside her. "While you were sleeping yesterday, I decided to go dig up worms. I know it's a big part of fishing."

"You?" Janie smiled.

"I marched myself down there and dug them up."

"With your bare hands?" Janie couldn't resist teasing Courtney just a little.

"I used a spoon."

"No gloves or anything?"

"Janie, please stop."

"Okay, I'm sorry."

"I had all I could do to keep from throwing up. But when Harold came along, I told him about my having to fish and your cooking. He offered to help."

"I didn't see the note you guys left. I'm sorry I yelled at you."

"Janie wait. There's something else."

Janie leaned back against the pillows. "Shoot."

"I don't know any boys, I mean like boyfriend boys. And Harold was being so nice to me . . ." Courtney took a deep breath, then let her words tumble out. "So, I pretended that he was my boyfriend. Do you hate me for that, Janie?"

Janie was quiet. She was surprised and not so surprised. She felt as if a long thread was quivering inside her. Obviously what she had been feeling the other night with Courtney and

Harold wasn't so crazy. Janie looked at Courtney. The thread quivered again. "It's okay, Courtney. I bet Harold loved it."

"Oh, Janie. You do understand! I really wasn't trying to get Harold from you."

"I know," Janie said. A long corridor opened within Janie. Bright light the color of laughter rushed down it, spilling out the other end.

"Ever since you got angry, I've been thinking I was going to lose your friendship."

"I don't want that to happen, Courtney."

"Me either, Janie. Not ever!"

14

———◆———

"Just grab a bagel," Janie said to Courtney as they headed downstairs. "You can eat it on the way."

"But where are we going, Janie?"

"Nowhere." Mrs. Tannenbaum greeted the girls as they entered the kitchen. "I was just going to call you. We need some help."

"What for?" Janie asked, but she had a very strong suspicion from looking around the kitchen.

"Today's the day. And you two are the official jam-stirrers."

"Groan," said Janie.

"Oh, come on, Janie." Courtney took over the pot on the left-hand burner. "It'll be fun." She climbed on a wooden stool and picked up a long-handled spoon.

Janie sat on the other stool. "Oh, all right."

"Your father just went up to take a shower. He'll be down in a little while. He's in charge of getting the wax on the jam. I have to run to the store for more sugar." Mrs. Tannenbaum picked up her tan cloth pocketbook. "Courtney, there's some omelet left in the fry pan for you."

"Thanks," Courtney said.

"I'll stir both pots while you eat." Janie stood in between the two simmering pots.

"Okay."

While Courtney made toast, Janie watched the fat blackberries slowly turning into a rich mush. "Boy, is this gross work."

"I'm sorry we didn't get to surprise your mother."

"I didn't want to learn how to cook anyway."

When Courtney finished eating, Janie handed back the spoon. "How can you tell when this stuff is done?"

Courtney held up the spoon watching the purple liquid drip down. "It's pretty close." She leaned over the pot, letting the sweet smell fill her nostrils. "I wonder what we'll be like when we're old ladies, Janie?"

Janie laughed. "I know."

"You do?"

"Sure, you'll still be gagging on worms, and I'll be living on candy bars." She stuck a spoon in the jam, then blew on it.

"You're right, I bet."

Janie licked her spoon. "We should promise to get together every year at the hospital just to see."

"I want to get together, but not there, Janie. That's all over, for us."

"You're right. So where's a good place?"

"Janie, we better do something about this jam or it's going to be overdone. The jars are there. You want to pour?"

Janie left her berries and found the potholders. Then carefully she and Courtney tilted the pot over the small glass jars. The jam rushed over the sides of the pot and onto the counter. It dripped in big slow plops onto the white linoleum floor.

"My mother's going to love her new purple floor," Janie said as she ran for the paper towels and a wet sponge.

Courtney tried to wipe down the counter with a cloth. "There has got to be a better way."

Janie tried dipping the jars into the pot next. That wasn't much better. The glass jars heated up too quickly to hold. Courtney had to fish them out with the spatula. Great gobs of sticky jam were hardening all over the countertops.

"I know," Courtney said, "let's try a soup ladle."

"Good thinking. Hey, what's that smell?" Janie spun around. On top of the stove a huge black cloud was rising out of the other pot. "You jerk!" Janie yelled at the electric range.

Quickly Janie dumped the pot into the sink and ran water over it. But it was too late. A second later, the smoke alarm over the door went off. Fang ran through the house barking.

"Janie, what do we do?" Courtney clamped her hands over her ears.

"I've got to get that alarm off. My father will kill me."

Janie dragged a chair across the floor and climbed onto it. "I can't figure out how!" She roared down at Courtney. "There's no place to turn it off."

Less than a minute later her father appeared. "What's going on?" he shouted as the alarm turned itself off. "What in the world . . . ?" He saw the kitchen.

On the counter was a blood bath of spilled jam. The walls and floor were spattered. A haze of smoke hung in midair.

Janie couldn't hear what he muttered as he lowered himself onto the chair. He sat there in his gray plaid bathrobe surveying the damage. "How long has your mother been gone?"

Janie looked at Courtney, who didn't know either. Janie shrugged.

"What were you trying to do?"

"Get the jam into those little jars."

"Wait till your mother sees this. We better get cracking."

But it was too late again. They all heard the car coming up the gravel driveway.

They only had one counter wiped clean when Mrs. Tannenbaum slammed the front door. "I'm home," she said before she reached the kitchen.

"Good God!" The brown paper bag sagged in her arms. "What's happened?"

"Well," said Janie picking at the sticky side of her face, "we were afraid it was going to burn."

"It's my fault; I didn't realize you were gone." Mr. Tannenbaum took the bags and put them on the table. "I was upstairs making a few phone calls."

Janie's mother's sandals stuck to the floor as she moved around. "It looks like you did surgery, not jam." Suddenly, she burst out laughing. "It serves me right. Wait till I tell my mother!"

"We'll clean up, Mom."

"No!" She looked around quickly. "Don't touch a thing. I'll be right back."

Mrs. Tannenbaum returned with her camera. "This has to be preserved." She looked at Janie. "No pun intended."

Mr. Tannenbaum groaned, but stood behind

Janie and Courtney as he was directed. They all smiled, including Fang, when the flashes went off.

It wasn't till afternoon that Janie and Courtney were able to get away. They hiked up the dirt road and through the overgrown apple orchard, stopping only long enough for Courtney to pick some wild daisies. She stuck the flowers in their hair.

At the top of the hill, Janie climbed over the wall. She watched Courtney, who only accepted a hand as she stepped back down. Then they trooped across the wooden bridge and passed the pond.

"Janie!" Courtney same to a halt. "Can we make a stop?"

"Sure."

"I want to see that loft you told me about the first day."

"Terrific. Let's go."

Janie ran ahead with Courtney close behind. The two were momentarily blinded when they stepped from bright sunlight into the dimness of the old barn. But Janie could hear the mice rustle toward hiding spots and the ducks take wing because of the intrusion.

"Ready?" Janie stood at the foot of the old ladder, nailed to a post.

"It looks steep."

"You can do it." Janie began to climb straight up. She stopped halfway. "Courtney, you okay?"

"Keep moving, Janie." Courtney sounded nervous. "I don't want to look down."

Janie reached the top of the ladder, and grabbing for a crossbeam, she hoisted herself over and onto the loft floor. There she waited for her friend.

Courtney refused help. Her face was flushed, but she made it. "I wanted to see if I could get up here."

Janie chuckled. "If you stay another week, you'll be jumping off mountains."

"No, thanks. Oh, Janie, the view!" Courtney moved to the window.

"I thought you'd like it."

Before them spread the lake in all its afternoon splendor. And even though it was still hot, the green trees were dotted with bits of orange and red.

"Boy, the summer's over," Janie said.

"I bet the sunset is beautiful from here."

"Hey, that reminds me. We better get going."

"I still don't know where we're going."

"Trust me," Janie said, as she disappeared down the ladder.

Courtney followed. They cut through a neighbor's yard and out onto the road. Together they marched across the field to the far side of the pasture.

Janie couldn't make herself walk, slowly. "This," she shouted back to Courtney, "is where we've been coming, all day."

Down near the trees were the two cows and the little calf. The baby was gamboling about, first rearing its hind legs, then trying to bolt over the walls.

"I've never seen a calf."

"I saw it born, last night."

"You did!"

"Come on!" Janie grabbed Courtney's hand. Together they raced down the hill, out of the sun and into the shade.

"You have to tell me all about it." Courtney was panting when they settled in the grass to watched the calf nurse.

"I will, I will. But you have to help me think of a good name."

"How about, Hey, Diddle-Diddle, since she likes to jump fences."

"That's as bad as my mother's suggestions." Janie stretched out on the grass, thinking and watching. She still had no ideas.

After she hung up the phone, Janie came back into her bedroom. "Harold can't come over. He's in some kind of trouble, I think."

Courtney stopped folding her blouse. "I wonder why?"

"His sister wouldn't tell me. She made it sound like a big deal."

"What could he have done?"

"All she said was Harold and his parents had a fight."

"I guess I won't get to say goodbye to him. Would you, Janie, for me?"

"Sure. In one way, I'm glad he can't come over."

Courtney looked puzzled. "You're not still angry about something?"

"No, not at all. But it's your last night here."

"I agree, but I'd like to have said so long." Courtney zipped up her case. "Well, I'm all done." She settled on the bed against the wall.

"Janie, what are you going to do about Harold?"

"What do you mean, *do*?"

"He really is your boyfriend, you know."

"What are you talking about?"

"If you got that upset with us the other day, I think it means something, Janie."

"Oh, yeah, like what?"

"Like maybe you do like him."

Janie bit on her thumbnail. "Don't you dare tell him."

"Janie, I wouldn't."

"And even if he is my boyfriend, I am not doing any junk stuff."

"What junk stuff is that, Janie?"

"Oh, come on, you know what I mean. Like

kissing in the movies and holding hands wherever you go."

"Who said you had to ?"

"Isn't that what you're supposed to do?"

"That's what I like."

"Well, there you go."

"Wait a minute, Janie. You don't have to do that, there's no rules!"

"What do you mean no rules? I know what dating's all about."

"Why couldn't you do things on your dates that you liked?"

"I don't know what you mean."

"Like fishing or playing baseball. It doesn't have to be a certain thing."

Janie leaned back. "Did anyone ever tell you, you're very smart."

"No, it just makes sense. Doesn't it?"

"Sure it does."

"Well then?"

Janie laughed out loud. "I wonder if Harold would like a cow-milking date? You've given me a great idea."

"Janie!" Mrs. Tannenbaum knocked, then opened the door. "You two should be getting ready for bed fairly early tonight. We have to be at the train station by eight."

"Okay," Janie said when her mother waved good night.

But they stayed awake talking for a long time,

about Courtney's swimming lessons, Janie's dates, and mostly about getting together at Christmas time. It was quite a bit later when they turned off the lights.

"Janie?" Courtney said in the darkness.

"Yeah?"

"You think you and Harold will be going steady by Christmas?"

"WHAT!" Janie pounded the wall.

"Only kidding, only kidding." Courtney tried to cover her giggles.

"You better be."

"Good night, Janie."

"Night."

"Janie, one more thing?"

"What?"

"Harold doesn't have a twin brother, by any chance?"

"No, just a gross sister."

"Being with him, I didn't worry about my back. I just had fun. You're lucky, Janie."

"I think so too."

"When I get home, I'm going to make up a questionnaire for a boyfriend. I want someone like Harold."

Janie fell asleep without any problems, but during the night she met the red glass bird again. He chased her down the long hallway of her dreams until she turned on him. "Listen you," she shouted, "I've had it. I'm not afraid of you. Get out of here."

The bird inched a step closer. His head was round like a basketball. His glued-on eyes were black on white paper.

"Hey, I mean it!" She stepped up to him. "You're nothing but a stupid toy that drinks from a cup." She began to laugh, and the more she laughed the smaller the bird became. When he was no bigger than her hand, he turned and fled.

15

They were late leaving the house the next morning, and reached the train station just in time. There were only a few seconds for a hug.

"Goodbye, I'll call you." Courtney waved from the train. "Thanks for the jam."

Janie waved and waved till Courtney was just a lavender dot moving down the track. Then she and Mrs. Tannenbaum climbed into the jeep.

"I feel so sad." Janie looked at her mother. "It was just starting to get really good again."

"So you worked things out with Courtney?" Mrs. Tannenbaum shifted the clutch.

"Harold, too."

"I'm glad."

When they reached the dirt road, Janie jumped out. She ran through the woods, uncertain of where Harold would be. Along the banks of the lake, she found only the early morning mist. And she did notice that the water had already started to drop. In a few spots she could see abandoned fish nests. They looked like shallow mud bowls. The geese circled in formation, getting ready for the flight south.

Janie turned and ran toward Harold's house. She found him sitting on the grass near the pine trees that divided his back yard from hers. He was playing his harmonica.

"I tried calling you last night, Harold. Courtney wanted to say goodbye." She sat down next to him.

"Yeah, I stopped over this morning, but your father said she'd already left."

"Yeah, we had to leave real early."

"Sorry, I missed her. I really wanted to read those books."

"She left them for you, and she gave me a really good idea."

"What?"

"Can you come to the barn later. You could read to the cows while I milk."

"Read to the cows!"

"Yeah, they like stories."

"Sounds crazy."

"You could even bring your harmonica and play for them. I'm sure they'd love it."

"That makes more sense."

"Try to come then."

"Okay, if I'm home from shopping for school clothes with my mother."

"Oh, grosso . . . hey, what happened at your house last night?"

"I told my parents, I didn't want to go to that camp."

"Whoa, Harold! You really did it. I can't believe it. What did they say?"

"At first they were upset, but we worked out a deal. They agreed to it—if I get a paper route."

"That sounds pretty good."

"Yes and no. The bad part is once I get my route then they stop giving me an allowance."

"Are you sure you don't want to go to camp, Harold?"

Harold smiled. "The good part is I can spend the money any way I want."

"Wow, that's really terrific. Now you'll be able to go on dates, and your parents won't stop you."

"I don't know if that's true, but I've changed my mind about dating. I've decided to save all my money."

"How come?"

"Well, for one thing . . ." Harold tilted his head. ". . . you ate up six months of my allowance in ice cream the other day, so I figure I can't afford it."

"Hey, I won that bet fair and square."

"Oh, I know, but if I go out on too many dates, then I won't be able to save any money."

"What do you have to save for? Are you buying a motorcycle or something?"

"Oh, no." Harold picked himself up slowly and began walking backwards across his yard. When he was close to his house, he yelled, "I'm saving my money to buy you an engagement ring."

"What did you say?" Janie jumped to her feet and charged after him.

But this time Harold was too quick. "I'm going to marry you, Janie Tannenbaum," he shouted and slammed the cellar door.

"HAROLD," Janie bellowed. "HAROLD!"

There was no answer. Janie stood in the middle of the lawn with her hands on her hips. Then all of a sudden she got the joke and fell down laughing. She stayed there till her sides ached and she could laugh no more. That's one for your team, Wazby, she thought. "See you in the barn," she shouted and started up the hill.

Janie ran over the hill with all the urgency of her nightmares and the freedom of her dreams. She didn't stop at the old stone wall to gaze at the trees laced with golds and reds. She didn't notice the breeze that whispered in the apple grove about the coming of winter.

Out across the pasture she rushed, but the cows were not around. So she followed the rocky stream, past the old metal bathtub filled with hay. Where are you, little calf, she thought, where are you?

That made her stop in her tracks. What were the words on the sign painted on the bridge railing? "Where are you, Cow Patty?"

Janie looked out over the hills. Down under the trees where the shade was, she saw the calf. "Hey," she shouted, "Cow Patty." Janie walked the rest of the way.